The London Rose

A REGENCY ROMANCE

ROSANNE E. LORTZ

MADISON STREET
PUBLISHING

Chapter One

Garden

Derbyshire, England
August 1810

M r. Gyles Audeley of Upper Cross in Derbyshire was an eccentric. While other young men of two-and-twenty were placing bets at Newmarket, buying boots from Hoby's, or escorting young ladies through Hyde Park, Gyles was observing the pollinating habits of bees and butterflies, constructing mechanical irrigation hoses, and propagating new species of roses.

No one denied that the roses were beautiful. They added a bloom of colour and a heady scent to the Audeley gardens and entranced everyone who walked the country lanes during the height of the hot weather. But even though she enjoyed the garden, Mr. Audeley's mother was quite certain that she would enjoy grandchildren more. And as matters currently stood, she despaired of Gyles ever leaving his garden long enough to find a wife.

In the autumn, he tended to the soil round the roses. In the winter, he pruned the roses back to a cluster of thorny stalks. In the spring, he planted new rose bushes and expanded the garden. And in the summer, he kept the bushes full by culling flowers past their bloom and cutting some to display throughout the house and in the village church.

"Gyles," Mrs. Audeley had said earlier this year, "should you like to take a house in London at the end of the summer? You would get to see the flowers at Kew Gardens and meet ever so many famous botanists. And I could perchance do some shopping—it's been four years since we were there last, just before your father died, you know—and I'm afraid I look quite the dowd."

She was too wise to mention young ladies, but the presence of them in London was the preeminent motivation in her mind. She knew that her son was of a romantic disposition, and if he could just be thrown in the way of some alluring young ladies, then love would take its course and all would be well.

Gyles, absorbed with his planting, had rubbed dirty hands on his old buckskins and squinted up at her. "I daresay *you* might take a house in London whenever you like, Mother. But I shall stay here in Derbyshire. Otherwise, who would take care of the roses?"

To no avail did Mrs. Audeley suggest local gardeners who might be employed instead of her son. He deemed no substitute acceptable for himself.

"And besides," he said, "one does not need to go to London to converse with famous botanists. Conversing by letter is much preferred. In fact, I have just had a letter from Sir Abraham Hume inquiring about the progress of the Sweet-Scented China Rose he sent me. I have great hopes that this will be the year the bush blooms."

And so, with that, Mrs. Audeley was forced to be quiet even though she was not entirely content. She waited out the spring and most of the summer as the Sweet-Scented China Rose was pruned and grew larger and put out leaves, and she watched for any eligible females who might be moving into the neighbourhood in Derbyshire. But the Audeleys' part of Derbyshire was a haven for established gentry families whose children had grown and gone, and while a few might come back with a bride and infants in tow, the eligible misses were in short supply. The nearest thing to an eligible female was Miss Morisson, the gentlewoman farmer two miles down the road, but as she was close to thirty, she was far too old for Gyles.

One day, when Mrs. Audeley was sitting down to a light nuncheon—alone, for Gyles was too engrossed in his gardening to come inside and share it with her—a quick rap came on the front door, almost frantic in its rapidity. Curious, Mrs. Audeley entered the hall. "I shall answer it," she said, forestalling Garrick, her butler. She adjusted her matron's cap and checked in the hall mirror to make sure that her nose had no smudges. It was not every day that an unexpected visitor came round to the front door in rural Derbyshire.

The visitor was a young woman with blue eyes as large and round as peonies. Her bonnet was halfway askew, and her black tresses were coming unpinned. Her white muslin dress was spotted with dirt about the shoulder and hip. And yet, she looked, on the whole, as if she must have been respectable when she first got dressed in the morning.

"Oh, I beg your pardon, madame," said the girl, her words coming out all in a tumble, "but I must beseech you to aid me in my hour of peril."

"Hour of peril?" asked Mrs. Audeley, a little bemused by such theatrics. "My dear child, what on earth can be the matter?"

"My guardian," said the girl, "a man filled with the greatest wickedness and moral turpitude, is riding in hot pursuit. I dare not fall into his clutches or disaster will befall."

"Dear me!" said Mrs. Audeley, clutching the girl's arm as she leaned against the doorjamb. She was a pretty young thing with an elfin chin and pert nose, far more in the style of a faerie child than an English beauty. "You must compose yourself, my dear. It won't do at all to have you fainting on the doorstep."

"Oh, thank you, madame. You *will* help me, won't you?"

Mrs. Audeley had only half a moment to consider. Being of a hospitable nature, she normally would have offered the girl a seat in the drawing room, a cup of tea, and a listening ear, but a thought occurred to her that this unexpected visitor might be Providence's answer to her hopes and prayers.

"I would offer you shelter, but I'm sure I should be far more successful in sending your guardian about his business when he arrives if I could tell him truthfully that I did *not* admit you to the house."

The girl gasped.

Mrs. Audeley hastened to soothe her. "But just around the corner of the house, there is a beautiful rose garden full of paths with twists and turns. I daresay you could hide yourself quite easily out there and wait in the shade until your guardian has gone. There might even be someone out there—a gardener, perhaps—who could find a pleasant bower for you to rest under."

Mrs. Audeley could see at once that the romantic nature of this solution appealed to the girl. "Oh, madame, that is counsel of the wisest sort! I shall do as you say and slip around to the garden." And with that the black-haired young lady recovered her energy surprisingly swiftly. She hurried around the corner of the house, treading lightly along the path in kid slippers that were not meant for walking great distances.

Mrs. Audeley stood a minute looking out the front door down the lane towards the main road that ran through their part of Derbyshire. How long would it be before the villainous guardian came in pursuit? And just how villainous would the brute be?

The butler, unused to having the front door standing open, cleared his throat just in case his mistress was daydreaming and need to be brought back to the moment.

"Garrick," said his mistress, still looking down the lane. "Take some lemonade for Mr. Gyles out by the pavilion. And bring two glasses."

"Yes, madame," said Garrick, a note of interest in his usually stiff voice. He departed to do her errand, and Mrs. Audeley closed the door and sat down in the drawing room to think.

Chapter Two

Guardian

I T WAS NOT AN hour before a knock sounded on the door again. This knock was less frantic and more imperious. "Ah," thought Mrs. Audeley to herself, "this must be the wicked guardian." And then aloud, she said, "Garrick, I am at home to guests."

From the nefarious description that the young lady had given, Mrs. Audeley was imagining an unpleasant fellow to appear. Likely balding. Probably snaggle-toothed. Doubtless belligerent. And definitely ruthless.

But after a moment ticked by on the long clock in the drawing room, Garrick showed in a gentleman who was none of these things. Mrs. Audeley sat frozen in utter silence as Garrick intoned, "His lordship, the Earl of Kendall."

Mrs. Audeley rose from her seat, trying to keep the pink of surprise from showing on her cheeks. To her knowledge, a member of the nobility had never set foot in her secluded manor house near Upper Cross. "The Earl of Kendall? To what do I owe the honour, my lord?"

The gentleman—for his top boots, pantaloons, and trim riding jacket proclaimed that he was unmistakably that—removed his riding gloves and slapped them against one hand. His black hair was flecked with grey, but he had the broad shoulders of a man in his prime and the air of one used to issuing commands. "Your butler tells me that you are Mrs. Audeley?"

"Indeed."

"I beg pardon for intruding. I was travelling near here on the main road. My ward, a Miss Penelope Trafford, was accompanying me in the carriage while I rode my mount alongside. When we stopped to water the horses, it became clear that somehow Miss Trafford had fallen out of the carriage, and so I've retraced our path to locate her."

"Fallen out of the carriage?" echoed Mrs. Audeley incredulously. Was this really the story he had decided to spread?

"Yes," said the man, his lips setting into a firm line. Mrs. Audeley did not realise that she had been admiring his faint smile until it disappeared completely. "And since your house lies quite near to the main road and there are no other houses of note within a mile, I thought she might have come here for aid."

Determined to make sufficient inquiry before admitting to anything, Mrs. Audeley gestured for Lord Kendall to be seated. "What is this, you say, about your ward falling out of the carriage? Are you certain she did not get out of the carriage on purpose?"

"Quite certain." Lord Kendall's boot heel tapped his impatience with the extraneous questions. "And I must ask you, madame, have you seen her?"

"I have been at home all day and have admitted no one to the house." It did not quite answer the question, but Mrs. Audeley lifted her chin as she said it and willed her voice to have conviction.

The tall man looked at her sharply, almost as if he had seen right through the evasion. Mrs. Audeley felt a blush creep out from her lace chemisette and up her neck. She could quite understand Miss Trafford's dislike of her guardian, or at least her discomfort in his presence.

"If you admitted no one to the house, might I beg the favour of examining the grounds?" He leaned forward in his chair like a large wildcat as if he were ready to spring up at a moment's notice.

"Whatever for?" Mrs. Audeley blinked her eyelids innocently as if she were too vapid to understand him.

His square chin set with irritation. "Perhaps Penelope was too confused to knock on the door of the house and found shelter elsewhere on the estate."

"Oh," laughed Mrs. Audeley. "I daresay someone would have come and told me if there were a young lady on the grounds. We live very quietly, Lord Kendall. The appearance of a young woman would have set all the servants by the ears."

"Nevertheless, I ask you to accommodate me. You would not want a young lady, frightened or injured, wandering your land if it were in your power to help her."

"N-no." Mrs. Audeley realised she could stall him no further in the drawing room. "Very well, I shall accompany you out to the gardens. Just wait a moment while I have a maid fetch my shawl."

"It is quite warm outside," said Lord Kendall pre-emptively, leaping from his chair as Mrs. Audeley rose to ring the bell. "I doubt you will be in need of a shawl."

"My parasol, then," said Mrs. Audeley. "It is so important to protect one's complexion when going out of doors in the summer."

They waited for several minutes while a maid brought Mrs. Audeley's pink parasol, but she declined it as being too sheer. Then they waited again while the maid searched for an Indian parasol which Mrs. Audeley had purchased long ago at a bazaar in London. It had been packed away in disuse for several years, but Mrs. Audeley had the happy notion that it would be the very thing for going out in this summer weather.

"Are you always this fastidious, madame?" asked Lord Kendall, his voice laced with sarcasm as he leaned against the drawing room wall, arms folded.

"I'm sure I don't know what you mean," said Mrs. Audeley. "Young ladies haven't a care in the world about their complexion, but we old ladies must be more cautious." For a woman just on the wrong side of forty, this description was almost laughable, but Lord Kendall made no demur at the way Mrs. Audeley chose to characterise herself. It was not very gallant of him, but she supposed that he was not in the mood for giving compliments to rustic widows working to thwart him at every turn.

They walked outside. Mrs. Audeley opened the parasol that the longsuffering maid had unearthed and sneezed delicately three or four times as it emitted a gentle shower of dust.

"I do hope you are not allergic to flowers," said Lord Kendall with a glint in his eye. They turned the corner into the gardens on the side of the house.

"I am not," said Mrs. Audeley, recovering herself.

"That is fortunate as this is the largest rose garden I have ever come across in this part of England."

"My son is an avid gardener. The cultivation of roses is his passion." Compared to the cosy manor house, the garden was immense. It was no wonder that the garden took up all of Gyles' physical and mental energies leaving nothing left over for the contemplation of matrimony.

"Ah." Lord Kendall's glance roved around the roses, his eyes trained over the top of the bushes rather than on the flowers themselves.

By this time, Mrs. Audeley had determined that since she was in for a penny she might as well be in for a pound. "You wished to see the grounds. Let me show them to you properly." Before he could protest, she took hold of his arm and gently indicated the direction they should go.

What followed was a circuitous half hour of wandering about the maze of rose beds. Mrs. Audeley stopped often to point out particular varieties and read off the names on the wooden placards that Gyles had designed.

Eventually, Lord Kendall extricated himself from her grasp and put a stop to their perambulation. "This horticultural tour is all very fascinating, but, Mrs. Audeley, I must ask you to bestir yourself a little and come to the point of our walk. Think now! Is there anywhere in the gardens that Penelope could be hiding herself?"

"Hiding?" said Mrs. Audeley, trying to fan herself with her empty hand. It was warm business walking so far when the sun was at its zenith. "Why on earth should she be *hiding* herself? I thought you said she had fallen out of the carriage accidentally?"

"A slip of the tongue," said Lord Kendall smoothly. "I mean, rather, is there anywhere she might be *resting* herself?"

Mrs. Audeley stared at him, at the moment truly befuddled from the heat.

A slight breeze struck up, ruffling the edges of the parasol and ends of Lord Kendall's hair. He lifted his chin and cocked an ear like a hound on the scent. "Listen. Do you not hear voices coming from that pavilion?"

"Voices?" Mrs. Audeley craned her neck as if trying to follow his lead. "I hear nothing, Lord Kendall. I daresay you are overheated and could stand to have some refreshment. Come, let us go inside and Garrick can serve us some lemonade."

"I would prefer to see the pavilion first."

"But *I* am overheated," said Mrs. Audeley, raising a hand to her brow and speaking in a tone of distress, "and I must beg you to assist me back to the house."

"My poor Mrs. Audeley!" said Lord Kendall. Without asking, he put an arm about Mrs. Audeley's waist to support her and took her other hand in his. Neither of them were wearing gloves, and the touch of his skin so startled and overawed her that she did not object. In a moment's time, she found herself being propelled towards the pavilion. It was unbelievably arrogant to move her about like a pawn on a chessboard, but she discovered that her knees truly were going weak and she had no strength left to oppose him.

"The pavilion will be just the place to sit down and recover yourself," Lord Kendall said reassuringly. He led her down the path and around the next bank of rosebushes. And there, they came in sight of a charming scene—a table under a shady pavilion, a pitcher of sparkling lemonade, and two young people deep in conversation.

CHAPTER THREE

Confrontation

"**P**ENELOPE TRAFFORD!" BOOMED LORD Kendall, his voice transforming in seconds from solicitous and urbane to rough and reprimanding. He relinquished his hold on Mrs. Audeley and strode into the pavilion.

The young lady in question shrieked loudly, abandoned her lemonade, and jumped from her chair to retreat to the back of the structure. Meanwhile, the young man—who was, of course, Gyles Audeley—rose as well and positioned himself in front of the young lady to shield her from her advancing guardian.

"So, you have found me at last, have you?" said Miss Trafford from behind her protector's shoulder. "You may have fooled everyone else with your false charm, but I see through it to the cold-hearted monster that you are. I refuse to be used for your own selfish purposes. Mark my words, Uncle, your time of tyranny is coming to an end."

"Oh my," murmured Mrs. Audeley, following Lord Kendall into the pavilion to see what was to be done. As she had hoped, the young lady had located her son in the garden, but she had not expected such a violent confrontation to occur once the young lady was found. How would her son respond to this fracas?

Incredibly, Gyles took his cue from the lady and broke out with an accusation of his own. "Stand back, villain! Penelope has told me of the wrongs done her, and I will not let you take her from this place."

Lord Kendall sighed in a tone that indicated he had been monstrously misunderstood. "Mr. Audeley...." He cast an inquisitive look at Mrs. Audeley who confirmed her son's identity with a nod. "I am not sure what tales my ward has been telling you, but let me assure you that her safety and wellbeing are very much my concern."

The four of them stood there in silence, the younger set glaring daggers at the earl while Mrs. Audeley swayed unsteadily. "Perhaps we might all sit down and discuss this in a civilised manner."

"Oh, but of course Mrs. Audeley. How remiss of me." Lord Kendall advanced to the table and pulled out a chair for Mrs. Audeley—whose cheeks were still pink from her excursion in the sun—while Gyles did the same, in a far more wary manner, for Miss Trafford.

"Now then," said Mrs. Audeley, taking Miss Trafford's hand and patting it sympathetically, "perhaps you both can tell us what this is all about."

"Miss Penelope Trafford," began Lord Kendall, "is the eldest daughter of my late sister Caroline—"

"I believe *I* should tell this part of the story," interrupted Penelope, "as she was *my* mother."

Lord Kendall paused. Mrs. Audeley could see annoyance pulsing through his strong jaw. But with an obvious show of effort, he gestured to his niece as if to say, "Be my guest."

"My dear mama Caroline along with my esteemed papa Henry died quite suddenly last year in a curricle accident, and no sooner did the news reach me and my sisters than the solicitor informed us that Mama's odious brother Lord Kendall was designated in the will as our guardian."

"Wait, my dear—how many of you are there?" asked Mrs. Audeley, who thought it an important detail to consider.

"Three," said Penelope with a sniff. "There is myself, Ginevra, and Camilla."

"Penny, Ginny, and Milly," interrupted Lord Kendall.

"Those are *not* the names by which you may refer to us!" said Penelope haughtily. "Our parents were not even three weeks in the grave when Lord Kendall required us to abandon the home we had always known and remove to the wilds of Yorkshire—"

"—which happens to be the location of my country seat," interjected Lord Kendall helpfully.

"And then no sooner did I become accustomed to that place than he tore me from the bosom of my sisters to bring me to the metropolis—"

"The other girls are joining us next month along with their new governess, Miss Lymington."

"—where he is determined to sell my hand in marriage to the highest bidder."

With this last comment, Miss Trafford's eyes began to well with tears. Gyles scowled indignantly at Lord Kendall and offered the weeping girl his handkerchief. She did not seem to notice that it had a bit of dirt on it from Gyles grubbing about in the flowerbeds earlier that day.

"And what do you have to say to that last charge?" asked Mrs. Audeley. She was feeling much more sure of herself now that she had a moment's rest, and she was quite pleased to see what an interest Gyles had taken in the young lady. Indeed, it was the most feeling she had ever seen him display about a *person*—although, to be truthful, he could become far more impassioned when discussing horticultural mishaps or his favourite plant species.

Lord Kendall frowned as he contemplated her question. Mrs. Audeley noticed that beneath those slanting brows he had the same arrestingly blue eyes that his niece possessed. "I am unsure where Penelope derived that last bit of information." He paused and looked at his niece wiping her pert little nose on Gyles' handkerchief. "However, I did tell her that I would be carefully interviewing any suitors who displayed an interest to make sure they were men of means. I have no intention of letting her fall prey to a fortune hunter."

"There, you see!" wailed Penelope. "He means to sell me off to one of his stuffy old friends, and I shall have absolutely no say in the matter!"

"'Pon rep!" growled Gyles in response. "It's absolutely monstrous of him!"

By this time, Mrs. Audeley was beginning to form her own opinion of Penelope's guardian and of Penelope herself. And while she did not think that Penelope was currently exhibiting the good sense that one would prefer in a daughter-in-law, she decided that such a fault was excusable in the recently bereaved and that Lord Kendall's avuncular manner left much to be desired.

"Am I to understand that you are taking Miss Trafford to London?"

"Yes, we are London-bound. Early for the season, but it will allow some time for my niece to have a new wardrobe made and acquire a little town bronze before the season starts in earnest." Lord Kendall hesitated, and then continued talking as if to make a clean breast of something. "In one of her last letters to me, Caroline indicated that she planned for Penny to make her come-out this year and had great hopes of her making a successful match."

At this, Penelope started to cry all the more. Mrs. Audeley was afraid that her red nose would render her a less romantic figure in Gyles' eyes. "My dear Miss Trafford, let us adjourn to the house where I'm sure we can discuss this in a more comfortable manner."

"You won't let him take me, will you?" pleaded Penelope.

"We shall explore all the options," said Mrs. Audeley diplomatically.

As Mrs. Audeley took Penelope's hand in hers and began to lead her down the path. The gentlemen followed behind at a discreet distance, Gyles eyeing Lord Kendall suspiciously and Lord Kendall exuding a coolness that defied the midsummer heat.

"So, you're a gardener, are you?" said his lordship, taking in the young man's dishevelled chestnut hair and rolled up shirtsleeves.

"Yes. What of it?"

"Not many young men of my acquaintance would have the patience for that sort of thing."

"It's quite easy when you see how beautiful the results can be," said Gyles. His indignation began to cool at this expression of interest in his favourite topic. "Keeping a picture of the summer garden in one's imagination allows one to endure the thorns and barren stalks of winter."

"Very poetic, Mr. Audeley." Lord Kendall's tone held dry amusement. How fitting that Penelope would find such a susceptible young man on which to pour her tale of woe. He could only hope that the young man's mother would see through his ward's machinations and send her about her business. At first, he had been afraid that Penny had completely won Mrs. Audeley over with tales about his villainy, but in the pavilion, she had seemed to display the glimmerings of sense.

With any luck, they would have a spot of tea and be on the road again in a quarter of an hour. And this time he would be riding *inside* the carriage with Penelope. He had no intention of playing hide-and-seek with her again before they reached London. And despite Penny's hysterics, one thing was for certain: he *would* do his duty by his sister Caroline.

Chapter Four

Resolution

WITH THE GENTLEMEN FOLLOWING several yards behind, Mrs. Audeley attempted to draw out the young
lady who had been cast so abruptly upon her doorstep. "How
did you escape from a moving carriage, Miss Trafford? It was
quite determined of you."

"Why, I threw both my half boots out the window into the
underbrush as we drove by, and it made such a racket when it
flushed out a pheasant that the coachman slowed down. My
uncle rode his horse over to the other side of the coach to investigate. And then, I slipped out the opposite door and hid in
the ditch until they went on by."

"Which explains the dirt on your gown." Mrs. Audeley said a
silent prayer of thanksgiving that she'd had only one mild-mannered son to raise and not a headstrong daughter like Miss
Trafford. "That was very resourceful of you."

"Thank you," said Penelope, recovering her buoyant spirits
as they walked. "I did feel heroic as I did it. Not quite the equal

of Isabella in *The Castle of Otranto*, but approaching something of that fortitude."

"Ah," said Mrs. Audeley, the picture of Penelope's influences becoming clearer now. "So you are a devotee of the Gothic novel."

"Yes, until Uncle Bertie forbade me to read them and took them all away."

It was clearly a tyrannical action, but in this case, Mrs. Audeley suspected it had been a wise one.

"Well, my dear, you must continue to exercise your bravery a little longer. A true heroine will not despair over a minor setback such as your guardian discovering your whereabouts. Have patience, and we will sort out this tangle to the good of everyone."

Once inside the house, Mrs. Audeley decided some sustenance was in order. She instructed Garrick to bring tea for everyone. She kept the conversation at a superficial level until each member of the group was fortified with at least one piece of teacake. Then, sensing Lord Kendall's impatience, she reintroduced the topic. "The afternoon is getting late. I believe we must return to the subject of what is to be done with Miss Trafford?"

"Oh, Mrs. Audeley!" said Penelope, clinging to the arms of her chair as if she were about to face the doom of Mary, Queen of Scots. "I can't bear to have him spirit me away from here. I shan't go to London! I shan't!"

Mrs. Audeley looked at Lord Kendall. "It *is* very soon after her mother's death to expect her to be launched into society. Do you have any female relatives in London who will be able to take her under their wing and guide her?"

"No, madame, I do not." His lips compressed into a line again as he looked at his overwrought niece. Then, he rose from his chair and began to pace beside the drawing room windows that overlooked the garden. "Caroline had planned to bring her out in the spring, but she was not ready then, so we stayed on in Yorkshire. I hoped the thinner company in town this autumn would provide an easier entry into society, so even though she baulked at coming once again, I insisted. I am only seeking to do what my sister Caroline would have wanted, but given Penny's infantile behaviour, I can see I might have acted prematurely."

Mrs. Audeley refrained from commenting. In her experience, when a gentleman was taking himself to task, it was best to leave the job to him.

Penelope, oblivious to her guardian's musings, continued her own lament aloud. "I shall be completely alone and friendless. It is *too* cruel!"

"Oh, surely not," said Gyles, leaning over to pat her arm. "We're your friends now, and we shan't let that happen."

"And how exactly do you propose to stop it?" asked Lord Kendall.

"Well, I shan't let her go to London all alone with you, for one."

"You really think I would allow a young pup like you to trail after us?" Lord Kendall raised an eyebrow. Mrs. Audeley could see that his patience with her quixotic son was wearing perilously thin.

"But that's a simply marvellous idea," said Penelope. "Why, if Mrs. Audeley and Gyles—that is to say, *Mr.* Audeley—were to go to London too, then I should feel ever so much safer and more comfortable. It is being left alone in a sea of strangers with only my unfeeling uncle that terrifies me."

"Yes, it would never do to be in London with *strangers*," said Lord Kendall, eyeing their new acquaintances with a sardonic curl to his lip. "I daresay you have known the Audeleys for all of two hours now."

"We have been talking about taking a house in London for the season," announced Gyles.

"Oh, have we?" murmured Mrs. Audeley, interested to see where this conversation was going.

"Why, yes, surely you remember, Mother? You most distinctly stated that you wished to enjoy the season and do some shopping so you don't look like such a dowd—"

Mrs. Audeley blushed and looked down at her faded green morning dress. She had had no opportunity to get new gowns made up for the last four years. But there was no reason for him to bring up *that* part of the conversation in front of their guests.

"—and I see no reason why we couldn't leave for town early, the same as Lord Kendall."

"But what about your roses?" said Mrs. Audeley, stunned by the suddenness of this decision.

"Garrick has a nephew roundabouts who can water and prune them well enough."

"But my dear! What about the Sweet-Scented China Rose which should bloom for the very first time this summer?"

Gyles paused. A look of supreme sacrifice came over his face. "I shall bring it with me."

"Oh," said Mrs. Audeley, equal parts shocked and delighted by this decision on her son's part.

"Oh!" squealed Penelope, delighted to hear that her plan was coming to fruition.

"Hmm," said Lord Kendall, narrowing his eyes, but he made no audible dissent to the notion.

"You won't get much farther down the road tonight," said Gyles, looking out the window, "so why not take supper here with us and spend the night and we can all start together in the morning?"

"Mrs. Audeley?" said Lord Kendall, putting the subject of their stay back in the hands of the mistress of the house. He stared at her intently.

"Yes, yes," she said, collecting her scattered thoughts. "It is no trouble at all. I will tell Cook to set for two more, and we shall make up two guest rooms."

Penelope turned to Gyles and the two began to chatter happily about what they would do when they reached London. Meanwhile, Lord Kendall moved quietly over to the chair where Mrs. Audeley was perched, fingering the green fabric of her dress in a distracted manner.

"I confess," he said in a low voice, "that this plan is entirely to my benefit, but I'm not sure that it is to *yours*. Are you certain that you were intending to come to London?"

Mrs. Audeley gave an uncertain smile. "Yes. Gyles may have overestimated how concrete our plans for travel were, but I had certainly *hoped* to visit London this year."

"And what will *Mr.* Audeley have to say about this adventure?" demanded Lord Kendall,

"He has already said he is well-pleased about the matter," said Penelope irritably, having overheard them from the other side of the room.

"I mean Mr. Audeley the elder."

"Ah," said Mrs. Audeley, apprehending his meaning a little more clearly. "My husband's feelings on the matter need not be consulted. He passed from this life four years ago."

"Hmm," said Lord Kendall, and his face took on an inscrutable cast. "Very well then, Mrs. Audeley. Since we are travelling in the same direction, we shall be delighted to be companions on the journey."

CHAPTER FIVE

Unearthed

I T WAS A DELICATE matter digging up and replanting a rosebush in the middle of summer, but Gyles rose early the next morning and with determination and a strong back, transferred the root ball, stalks, thorns, leaves, and burgeoning buds into a large pot. With the help of Garrick's nephew and two of the footmen, the pot was levered into motion and soon took pride of place in the Audeleys' travelling carriage. Two black horses, handsome but not particularly fast goers, were harnessed to the carriage-turned-plant-nursery.

"I was hoping that I could ride with you," said Penelope, a little downcast as she saw how much room the rosebush took up in the carriage.

"I beg your pardon," said Gyles, "but I shall need to keep a strict eye on the rosebush to make sure it does not dry out as we travel." It was not a gallant thing to say, but a gardener cannot always be gallant when a transplanted specimen from an exotic clime is at stake.

"It seems that you are bringing your own acreage from Derbyshire down to London," said Lord Kendall, looking at the giant pot of dirt with amusement.

"Yes, I did tell him to lay down an oilcloth on the carriage floor," said Mrs. Audeley, shaking her head at the enormity of the pot, "but it looks as if that instruction was missed. I hope that he does not intend to water it while in transit."

"How would it be," said Lord Kendall as if the muse had just struck him, "if *you* were to ride in *our* carriage, Mrs. Audeley? I know Penny would be glad of the company."

"How delightful!" Mrs. Audeley beamed. Her hand smoothed down her dove grey travelling dress, slightly out of fashion but one of the smartest outfits in her wardrobe. "I must confess, I was not looking forward to snagging my skirt on prickles and thorns each time the coachman pulled up hard on the reins."

And so it came about that Mrs. Audeley and Penelope passed a very pleasant morning on the road from Derbyshire. Mrs. Audeley regaled Penelope with tales of her own come-out in England, twenty-four years ago. "Of course, dresses and hair were much larger back then. Can you imagine wearing panniers that made you turn sideways to enter a drawing room?"

"Goodness! How quaint it all must have been," said Penelope, who knew nothing more of fashion than the high-waisted frocks and narrow skirts that were currently worn.

They stopped for lunch at a wayside inn chosen by Lord Kendall and sat down to a hearty meal of bread, vegetables, and beef stew. Gyles and Penelope made faces at each other over the bitter ale, but Lord Kendall would not let them have any of the sole bottle of claret that the innkeeper had unearthed and insisted instead upon Mrs. Audeley having two glasses.

"I shall fall asleep in the carriage immediately after such a fine meal," said Mrs. Audeley, stifling a yawn, as they walked back out to the carriage.

"I daresay Penny can talk enough for two," said Lord Kendall breezily. Penelope glared frostily at him, but he ignored her and tied his horse to the back of the equipage. When she realised that he meant to ride inside with them, her glare intensified, but they had not gone half a mile down the road before Mrs. Audeley started sharing her stories again and put the girl in a better mood.

"How frightening your court presentation was, Mrs. Audeley. And just think, Uncle Bertie, how funny the men must have looked with heels and jewelled buckles on their shoes."

"You forget, my dear Penny, that Mrs. Audeley and I are much of an age and that *I* was one of those silly gentlemen with jewelled buckles on my shoes. I do believe my hair was whiter then than it is now."

"Oh goodness!" shrieked Penelope. "Did you powder your hair?"

"Aye, and wore it long tied back in a queue." He grinned at his niece. "But I never wore patches or rouged my cheeks."

"I should think not!" said Penelope, far too used to her odious staid uncle with closely cropped black hair to imagine him as some sort of decadent courtier. "Did you know Mrs. Audeley when she had her come-out?"

Lord Kendall looked at Mrs. Audeley as if he were considering that question for the first time.

"I am sure that your uncle and I did not move in the same circles. He is of a far more exalted status, and I was simply Miss Trimble of Upper Cross."

"But Upper Cross is where we found you," mused Lord Kendall, "so it seems you did not travel far after your season in London."

"No." Mrs. Audeley tucked the brown curl that had come loose from her cap back underneath where it belonged. "I went to London and had my season, and then I came home and married Mr. Audeley of Upper Cross, just as my family had suspected would happen all along."

"Whereas Uncle Bertie never married at all," said Penelope spitefully, "as no one would have him."

"I rather doubt that was the reason," said Mrs. Audeley in gentle reprimand, but Lord Kendall simply raised an eyebrow at his niece and turned his attention out the carriage window. Which left Mrs. Audeley to ponder the question: why was it that Lord Kendall had never married? He certainly had the money, title, looks, and address to attract a wife. And yet, he must be a few years past forty and still a bachelor.

Perhaps there was some long-lost love in his youth that he could not forget. Or perhaps he simply had no taste for the settled life of family. But whatever the case, family life had certainly been thrust upon him unseasonably. He was now the guardian to three lively girls and had the unenviable duty of launching them into society. As a single gentleman without female relatives to aid him in the planning, he would need all the help he could get.

CHAPTER SIX

Ices and Lodgings

A FTER THREE DAYS OF travel, during which Lord Kendall oversaw every halt and meal and inn and change of horses, the Audeleys and their new friends arrived in London. Lord Kendall had made arrangements for his townhouse to be aired and opened in advance of their arrival, but the Audeleys—with their journey being so impromptu—had not yet found apartments to let.

"How vexing it is that you cannot stay with us," said Penelope, still perplexed about the inconvenience that was propriety. "Uncle Bertie's house is far too large for just the two of us. You must find somewhere close by, for I *must* have you by my side, Mrs. Audeley, at all times. I quake to think of being thrust into an assembly or a soirée with only my uncle as a chaperon."

"We shall do our best to find something in proximity," said Mrs. Audeley, but inside she was not optimistic. No doubt all the best places had already been snatched up for the autumn by those who had the foresight to let lodgings ahead of time. And although Mrs. Audeley was not impecunious, she did not have the limitless funds that the Earl of Kendall clearly possessed.

Lord Kendall gave Mrs. Audeley the address for an elegant hotel along with a note of recommendation from himself to the proprietor. The maître d' took one look at the note and ushered her into a luxurious suite of rooms with marble floors and gilt chandeliers. Mrs. Audeley sighed with delight, feeling as if she were in Paris, not London. Gyles remained unaffected by the luxury, having little appreciation for beauty that was not of the organic variety.

On the following day, Mrs. Audeley took the carriage to see her solicitor while Gyles installed his rosebush in the courtyard atrium attached to the Kendall townhouse. "I will visit it every day," said Gyles, carefully examining the buds that had already formed to ensure that the shock of transplanting it had not damaged them in some way.

Lord Kendall took the matter with good grace. "I suppose since you have uprooted yourselves to come to London at my niece's request, housing your rosebush is the least I can do."

Penelope and Gyles spent a pleasant morning playing piquet—although Gyles soon discovered that, to keep the peace, it was best to let the lady win. Round about noon, Mrs. Audeley returned from the solicitor's office and came in the carriage to collect Gyles at the Kendall townhouse. As she waited in the entrance hall, she was quieter than normal, and a look of care had come into her clear brown eyes.

Sensing that something was amiss, Lord Kendall suggested a luncheon outing and whisked them all away to Gunter's so that an assortment of flavoured ices could help them all bear the sweltering late summer heat of the capital.

"This parmesan ice is delightful," said Penelope with a sigh.

"I much prefer the lavender," said Gyles, who had made trial of them all.

"You seem perplexed, Mrs. Audeley," said Lord Kendall, drawing her away from the younger members of their party over to their own private table.

Mrs. Audeley sat down with an apologetic sigh. "Oh, I have been talking to Mr. Mulgrave, my solicitor. He is going to make inquiries about a lodging place for us, but he was not at all optimistic. The best places, he said, are all secured months in advance. It is quite unlikely we'll find anything in Mayfair for lease, and all the available properties he knows of are quite close to the river—"

"—which is unacceptable due to the stink." Lord Kendall nodded sympathetically.

"Yes." Mrs. Audeley adjusted her bonnet which, now that she was in London, seemed even more outmoded than it had in Derbyshire. "I must confess, our decision to come to London might have been made too hastily and without proper planning."

"My dear Mrs. Audeley," said Lord Kendall, "I am indebted to you for making such a sacrifice, and I promise you I shall investigate the matter and help you find lodgings to your satisfaction. In the meantime, the hotel is not too uncomfortable, I trust?"

"Oh no!" said Mrs. Audeley. "One does not like to complain about the softest of featherbeds and a divine cup of chocolate in the morning." She would not, for all the world, have Lord Kendall think she was displeased with the hotel he had recommended. "It is just that one likes to have a place of one's own to fully unpack and feel at home."

She was also fully aware that the hotel was an expensive one. The more nights they spent there, the larger the bill would be when they left.

Lord Kendall took another pistachio ice from the waiter and gave it to Mrs. Audeley with firm instructions to eat it before it melted. "I know just what you mean. I have a great aversion to staying anywhere besides one of my own houses in London or Yorkshire."

Mrs. Audeley nodded, trying to keep her own thoughts in check. Before they left, she instructed Gyles to pay a shilling from his purse for the ices.

"I shall take care of it," said Lord Kendall.

"No, no," objected Mrs. Audeley. "You were far too generous on the journey to London. Now that we are here, we shall pay our own way."

After their luncheon at Gunter's, the two parties took their leave of one another, with Mrs. Audeley promising to call on the morrow to take Penelope shopping. However, that evening, she was surprised to see Lord Kendall approach them in the dining room at the hotel with news of a nature that could not wait.

"I've had my man of business look into the matter, and he's found a vacant townhouse on Green Street, just around the corner from Grosvenor Square. Should you like to see it this evening?"

"Oh, yes!" said Mrs. Audeley who did not like the sun to go down on a task that could be completed that day. Gyles did not quite understand the urgency, but Lord Kendall bundled him into the carriage, and they were off to Green Street while there was still light to properly examine the place.

"What do you think?" asked Lord Kendall after they had toured the dining room, drawing room, library, and bedrooms.

"It seems adequate," said Gyles. He was more interested in the small garden plot neatly wedged beside the stable and carriage house and was busy calculating whether the soil had suitable drainage.

"The question was addressed to *Mrs.* Audeley," said Lord Kendall. "A young buck like you can stay anywhere that has a sofa and a larder."

"It is very well-situated and well-appointed," said Mrs. Audeley. "The walls and furnishings have all the marks of excellent taste, and I particularly like the light from the large windows in the drawing room." A thought came to her which sent a line between her brows. "But is it out of my reach? How expensive must a place so close to Grosvenor Square be?"

Lord Kendall leaned against the blue and white paper that decorated the wall. He folded his arms. "How much were you hoping to spend?"

Mrs. Audeley flushed, for although she was prudent with her shillings and pence, she had not had time to make a clear reckoning of how deeply this London trip would decimate her savings. "I daresay that I should not like to go above twenty pounds for the season. But is that far too small a sum for a house in this location? I know nothing of what houses may cost in town." Mrs. Audeley clasped her hands in dismay. "And it is furnished, which must make the price all the higher."

"Twenty pounds will be quite sufficient," said Lord Kendall, reassuringly. "I shall have my man of business see to it with the owner. You can move in tomorrow."

"Oh!" Mrs. Audeley's eyes opened wide. "How marvellous."

The search for lodgings had been far more successful than she could have ever dreamed.

And yet, had she known that the owner of the house was, in fact, the very man she was talking to, and that furthermore, he had purchased the house with her in mind that very afternoon, she might have been more dismayed than satisfied with the serendipitous arrangement of her affairs.

CHAPTER SEVEN

Shopping

MRS. AUDELEY SPENT THE morning unpacking at her new residence. Her coachman and one of the footmen had come down from Derbyshire with them, but now that the residence was secured, she sent a message for Garrick, Cook, and two of the maids to come south by the post, leaving only a skeleton staff at Upper Cross to care for the empty house and grounds. Lord Kendall might have separate staff for country and town, but she was not prepared to pay double wages when one house was not in use.

Gyles walked over to Lord Kendall's house in the heart of Grosvenor Square and came back an hour later filled with worry. He sat down heavily on the new claw-footed sofa and put a hand to his brow. "The sepals of one of the buds have grown most alarmingly yellow. Oh, Mother! I fear the worst."

Mrs. Audeley laid down the spencer she was folding and commiserated with him. Although her attachment to that particular rosebush was far less ardent than his, she *had* seen him in a fever of botanical depression before. It was not pleasant, and she wished to avoid a complete case of the dismals if possible.

"I must call on Sir Abraham Hume," declared Gyles.

Mrs. Audeley affirmed the wisdom of that plan and immediately offered him use of the carriage. "It is high time you met the man after corresponding with him for so many years. Shall you mind, then, if I go shopping with Penelope without you?"

"Certainly not. And I must say how pleasant it is for Lord Kendall to take on the task of escorting you ladies so I shall not be taxed with it."

"That is not very gallant. I daresay Penelope would be quite put out if she learned you were only happy to protect her from her guardian when milliners' shops are not involved."

"Oh, do you think I ought to come then? I must confess, on our trip here, Lord Kendall lulled me into thinking that he is not quite as terrible as Miss Trafford describes. But she says his affability is all a front and that I must not be taken in. If you think my presence is required—"

"No, no," said Mrs. Audeley, aware that her teasing had gone too far. "I shall be able to ensure Miss Trafford's safety quite well on my own." In fact, from previous experience, she recognised that her presence would actually be more of a shield and buckler for Lord Kendall. Penelope was so ready to savage her uncle at the least provocation, and Mrs. Audeley was unconvinced that he was deserving of so much hostility. Hopefully, she could be a restraining influence on the young lady.

"We shall divide and conquer," said Mrs. Audeley. "You tend to your rose, and I shall tend to Penelope."

"Thank you, Mother," said Gyles with relief. "She *is* a lovely girl, is she not?" He stared at the moulding of the ceiling in rapt contemplation—like Dante on his muse Beatrice.

Mrs. Audeley said nothing. She dared not interrupt his reverie.

"But," he continued after a moment, "there is something exhausting about being in her presence for more than an hour or two. I don't know how you bore the entire carriage ride from Derbyshire with her. I was quite glad I had my rosebush to distract me." And with that, he disappeared to locate the address for Sir Abraham while Mrs. Audeley was left to ponder that her son's infatuation with the girl he had met in the rose garden was not as deep as it had first appeared.

Lord Kendall was just as prepared for the shopping excursion as he had been with the housing arrangements. Mrs. Audeley discovered that he had made appointments for both her and Penelope at one of the most exclusive modistes in London. It was a kind consideration. She had not expected it. Her previous experience shopping in London had involved hunting for bargains in the less elevated shops along Bond Street. The thought of having the exclusive Madame DeLaittre fit her for gowns was a dream made of Chantilly lace.

Once inside the shop, Lord Kendall took up a position in a chair by the door reserved for disinterested gentlemen. He opened a copy of *The Sporting Magazine*, but a close observer might have noted that his eye was far more interested in the spectacle before him than the printed page.

Mrs. Audeley chose her fabrics swiftly with an eye toward price and durability. She already had an idea what colours complimented her brown hair and light olive skin—amber, purple, chocolate, and moss green. A few discreet questions to the shop assistant revealed that the modiste's fees were higher than she was used to, so she abbreviated her shopping list to no more than two morning dresses, two walking dresses, and an evening gown.

"Come now, Mrs. Audeley, you must have a ball gown," said Penelope.

"Oh, I do not think at my age it is necessary."

"But I am to have a come-out ball," said Penelope, "and everyone must dance at it!"

At that, Mrs. Audeley saw reason and allowed the modiste to show her sketches for a marvellous ball gown in burgundy silk. It was very dear, but Penelope insisted that she would look divine in it. "For even though you are ever so much older than me, Mrs. Audeley, you still have the figure for it."

Mrs. Audeley smiled good-naturedly, the laughter lines around her eyes being the only detectable evidence of her age. But even though she agreed to the addition of a ball gown to her order, Lord Kendall detected a pinched look about the forehead when she thought herself immune from observation. And later, he overheard her cancelling the order for one of the walking dresses that had previously been decided upon.

Penelope, on the other hand, had no qualms about expense. She was under the quite accurate impression that Lord Kendall would pay for anything and everything her heart desired. He was under a sacred obligation to her late mother to make her a success in the eyes of the ton, and she was determined to take full advantage of that obligation.

At first, the young woman was drawn to necklines and trimmings that were not at all suitable to her girlish frame. Lord Kendall had the good sense to say nothing when she reached for the purple bombazine or red crape, as that would only have set her back up. But with Mrs. Audeley's tact and Madame De-Laittre's good taste, Penelope was steered away from anything that was too gauche or too old for her. In the end, she came away with orders for a dozen and a half gowns, two pelisses, two spencers, an Indian shawl, three sets of gloves, two sets of stays, five chemises. In addition to this, she selected several pairs of dancing slippers and some new half boots—as hers had disappeared into the roadside bushes of Derbyshire.

"Ginny and Milly will be ever so jealous when they arrive," Penelope said, chattering happily in the carriage after they left the shop.

"Their time will come," said Lord Kendall, affecting a tone of longsuffering saintliness. Mrs. Audeley caught his eye and he smiled ruefully. She reflected that it must be a lowering thought for him that every experience and expense would eventually be multiplied by three.

"I daresay you are bored to death of our frocks and furbelows," said Mrs. Audeley, "and of the indecision which must savour each selection."

"Not at all," said Lord Kendall gallantly. "I know that furnishing yourself with a new wardrobe was one of your main reasons for coming to the capital, and I appreciate a pretty woman in a new dress as much as the next man."

The compliment was given so gaily that Mrs. Audeley was able to receive it without blushing, but later she reflected that Lord Kendall—should he desire it—was quite able to turn a lady's head if she did not keep it squarely on her shoulders.

CHAPTER EIGHT

Accomplishments

I T WAS TOO SOON for Mrs. Audeley's cook to have arrived from Derbyshire, so Lord Kendall insisted that the Audeleys dine with them in Grosvenor Square each night until their domestic arrangements settled into normalcy. Tonight, Gyles was there ahead of them, in a brown study contemplating the rosebush in the courtyard atrium.

"What does Sir Abraham say?" asked Mrs. Audeley.

"Why, other than that I am a young blockhead to think of transplanting a rosebush in the heat of summer, he says that I must be patient. It may take several weeks to recover from the shock. And I must continue to water it well and clip off any leaves or buds that look sickly."

"That is very sound advice," said Mrs. Audeley, relieved to hear that there was some hope. As much as she had wanted to come to London, she would have been sad to think that it had been accomplished at the expense of something so dear to Gyles.

They removed to the dining room, Lord Kendall taking Mrs. Audeley's arm and allowing Gyles to do the same for Penelope. Rather than utilising the whole of the long dining table, Lord Kendall had ordered for their seats to be placed all together on one end.

"I hope the salmon is to your satisfaction, Mrs. Audeley?" inquired her host.

"Oh yes," said Mrs. Audeley. "It is not possible to get such fresh fish in Derbyshire."

"Another advantage that London has over the country."

After the evening meal was consumed, they removed to the drawing room—neither of the gentlemen standing on ceremony to linger over port—and Mrs. Audeley noted that the room was quite as large as four of her own drawing rooms put together and contained an elegant pianoforte in one corner of it.

"Shall we have some music?" asked Gyles, looking at Penelope hopefully.

"Oh, I do not play," said the girl, looking as appalled as if he had asked her to stand on the back of a moving horse at Astley's Amphitheatre.

"Yes," said Lord Kendall, wryly. "It appears my sister was not in the habit of requiring her daughters to develop any accomplishments that require discipline. I have since rectified that by engaging a governess—although in Penny's case, it is a matter of *too little, too late*."

Penelope shot her uncle a barbed glance and would have followed it with a verbal volley, but Mrs. Audeley intervened. "I have often observed that young ladies who do not play the pianoforte are gifted in singing. Do you like to sing, Penelope?"

"Well enough, when I know the song."

"Let us see then if your uncle has any sheet music you know." Mrs. Audeley hurried over to the shelf by the piano and after a moment's perusal found some Irish airs that Penelope recognized.

Mrs. Audeley sat down at the pianoforte to accompany her, and Penelope made her way through the piece quite creditably. Her voice had an untrained, girlish timbre to it, but even a jaded observer must have acknowledged that it was sweetly in tune. When she finished the piece, Gyles applauded enthusiastically and even Lord Kendall's praise came unsought.

"Mrs. Audeley certainly seems to know how to bring out the best in you." Lord Kendall looked at their guest thoughtfully.

Mrs. Audeley's hands dropped from the keys of the pianoforte to settle in her lap. After running her hands over the expensive silks and satins at the modiste's earlier that day, she could not help but feel that her old round gown in cream muslin was woefully shabby.

No doubt Lord Kendall felt the same, for she could not think of any other reason why his eyes would continue to linger on her long after the music had stopped.

Rising from her seat at the pianoforte, Mrs. Audeley returned to where the gentlemen were sitting and joined Penelope on the sofa. "What do you think, Mrs. Audeley?" asked Lord Kendall. "Could you also participate in our campaign to secure invitations for Penny when the season starts?"

"Why must we do that?" demanded Penelope. She seemed unaware that invitations did not fall like manna from heaven the moment a young lady desired them."

"We must acquaint the ton with the fact that you are *here*, and hopefully provide them with the impression that you are not an unmannerly *hoyden*."

Penelope opened her mouth to let out a complaint of being ill-used, but Mrs. Audeley pressed her hand and urged her to wait and hear out her uncle's plan.

"I was thinking we might hold a small dinner party, just a few old friends, and of course, our new friends the Audeleys, so that you might practise being in company."

"You must invite young people too. I shan't put up with you foisting your fusty old friends on me, no matter how much money they have."

Lord Kendall's nostrils flared. He took a deep breath as if to gain control of his emotions. "I daresay I can find some people of a suitable age to entertain you. Although Mrs. Audeley and I may prefer conversing with old relics as we are so much closer to being in our dotage." He turned to his guest. "You must let me know, Mrs. Audeley, if there is anyone of your acquaintance that you would like me to include."

And then returning his attention to Penelope, he issued the final word on the matter. "We shall set a date for one week from now. Some of your new gowns should have arrived by then, and it will give our guests time to respond to the invitation."

Afterwards, when Gyles and Penelope had moved to the table on the other side of the expansive drawing room to play spillikins, Lord Kendall took the place Penelope had vacated on the sofa next to Mrs. Audeley. "Thank you," he murmured.

"For what?" Mrs. Audeley asked in surprise.

"For saving me from losing my temper. You are very good with her, you know. I have no...experience with children."

Mrs. Audeley laughed at that. "I have no experience with children of this kind either. Gyles was so mild-mannered as a child that he rarely gave me the need to take away his toys or ring him a peal."

She hesitated and then looked frankly into Lord Kendall's deep blue eyes. "I *think* that most of Penelope's histrionics stem from her recent loss. To lose one's mother and father in one fell swoop is an unfathomable blow, especially for a girl on the cusp of womanhood. When she sees you, it is not her uncle that she sees, but someone taking the place of the people who *should* be there for her. And so she strikes out blindly with her tirades and her tantrums. But in her heart of hearts, I believe she hopes that someone will take her flailing arms calmly and firmly and stop her from doing a mischief to herself or to others."

Lord Kendall leaned in closer, his voice low and gravelly. "That is a very sensible synopsis of the situation, Mrs. Audeley. I shall endeavour to keep it in mind when she provokes me beyond all patience."

His intense stare continued after he had finished speaking, and Mrs. Audeley was flustered enough that she pulled her attention away and fiddled with the lace cap on top of her brown curls. "One hopes that Ginevra and Camilla are less taxing?"

"Ginny and Milly are certainly less taxing, but each is perplexing in her own way." He smiled and raked a hand through his close-cropped dark hair, sprinkled with flecks of grey. "You shall see, Mrs. Audeley, when they come to London next month, and I daresay you shall give me sound advice on how to get on with them too."

CHAPTER NINE

Lions

T HE NEXT WEEK FLEW by in a flurry of activity. Lord Kendall engaged a French maid named Jeanette to add sophistication to Penelope's appearance. "She is awfully good at dressing my hair," Penelope confided in Mrs. Audeley, "but I can never dispel the feeling that she is sneering at me behind my back. Is it the same with your maid, Mrs. Audeley?"

"No," said Mrs. Audeley, sympathetically, "but I merely ring for one of the housemaids to lace my gowns, and I dress my hair myself. You are fortunate to have such an accomplished maid, and I daresay you'll grow used to her within the week and will never want to be parted from her."

Penelope had never been to London before, so Lord Kendall treated them all to several outings—the Tower of London, Astley's Amphitheatre, and even Kew Gardens on a day that was not too warm.

Mrs. Audeley's new walking dresses had arrived from the modiste—both of the ones that she had ordered although she was certain that she had made it quite clear that the moss green dress must be cancelled. When she had asked to see the bill, however, it was much lower than she expected. She supposed she must have been mistaken about the initial price and, since she was not obliged to send one of them back, now had the pleasure of two options to choose from on their outings.

On the morning that they visited the menagerie at the Tower, Lord Kendall asked, "You must have been to all these places, Mrs. Audeley, when you had your season?"

"Yes," said Mrs. Audeley, "although Mr. Audeley was not fond of London, and we rarely came to town after I married." She wrinkled her nose at the smell coming from the animal cages, quite content to look from afar while Gyles and Penelope advanced closer to the metal bars.

Lord Kendall hung back beside her. "How is it that you met Mr. Audeley?"

"I had known him all my life in Derbyshire. He came from an old family in Upper Cross. Very respected." She peeped up Lord Kendall from beneath the brim of her bonnet. It was a new one with white trim, the single hat she had allowed herself to purchase on one of their subsequent trips to Bond Street, and she was pleased to have one bonnet that she need not be ashamed of. "I suppose Mr. Audeley was what Penelope would call one of my father's 'fusty old friends.' He was nearer to my parents' age than mine. My father was a solicitor and Mr. Audeley was one of his clients."

She would have left it at that, but when she fell silent, Lord Kendall jumped in to finish the story for her.

"So, you grew up with Mr. Audeley staying to dinner whenever he had business with your father. Then one day you were no longer there at dinner because you were in London enjoying your season, and he realised how much he had come to enjoy your company and that you were a woman grown...."

Mrs. Audeley blushed. It was mortifying to hear Lord Kendall describe her life as if he were looking in on it from a storefront window.

"...You had your six months of gaiety in London but met no one you liked better than Mr. Audeley. And when you returned to Upper Cross you discovered that he was there waiting for you."

"Something of that nature," Mrs. Audeley replied faintly, "although, to be sure, it is a much longer tale." The way Lord Kendall described it, her first marriage had been decidedly romantic, when the truth was, it was anything but—

From ten yards away Penelope let out a scream. Lord Kendall's chin lifted sharply, and his eyes ranged across the courtyard. He relaxed instantly when he saw she had just been frightened by the sight of the mangy lion inside its cage.

"That moth-eaten carpet could hardly rise to its feet let alone attack a vigorous young lady like Penelope." He arched an eyebrow at his niece, hiding herself behind Gyles' back while the young man puffed out his chest like a male partridge.

"What is it your son sees in her, I wonder? A helpless innocent to protect?"

"Isn't that what all gentlemen hope to see in a woman?" Mrs. Audeley tried to keep the traces of pain out of her voice. "A pretty armful who hangs upon their every word as if it were from the fount of wisdom and relies on them for every choice or challenge."

"No."

"No?"

"No." said Lord Kendall decisively. "That is not what every gentleman hopes to see."

Penelope gave another squeak of terror and clutched at Gyles' arm.

"And in this case, one would hope that Gyles is not one of those gentlemen. Appearances can be deceptive. Penelope loves to pretend terror, but she is staunch as a soldier when the need arises. Should that flea-bitten lion actually tear through the bars of the cage, I daresay she would stand her ground and brain him with the heel of her half boot."

Mrs. Audeley tilted her head to look up at him. "I daresay you have the right of it. Penelope is intrepid. At her age, I would never have had the audacity to stand my ground to a lion—or a guardian."

Lord Kendall offered Mrs. Audeley his arm so they could join the young people. "I find that the older I become, the less fearsome the lions are."

"Indeed, although sometimes the lions in one's imagination grow more fearsome the longer they linger."

"I wonder—what lions lurk in *your* imagination, Mrs. Audeley?" asked Lord Kendall softly.

But Mrs. Audeley only smiled brightly and said, "Look at the monkeys!" and the whole group went off in the direction of another exhibit and let sleeping lions lie.

Chapter Ten

Friends

L ord Kendall's campaign to give Penelope some town bronze commenced the following week. The dinner party at Kendall House was arranged to have no fewer than twelve guests. Lord Kendall introduced Miss Trafford as his ward and also introduced Mrs. Audeley and her son Mr. Audeley as new friends from the countryside. Sir Oliver Comfort and Lady Arabella Comfort occupied the dreaded position of being *old* friends of the earl, but they had two daughters who were close in age to Penelope and fit her demands for youthful company quite nicely. Mr. Heller and Mr. Tavinstock, both young men with convivial spirits and impeccable reputations, were invited to enliven the young ladies. And finally, a Mr. and Mrs. Haverstall joined the party—very distant acquaintances of the Earl of Kendall but known particularly to Mrs. Audeley.

Mrs. Audeley wore her new evening gown of chocolate brown silk. The wide neckline left her shoulders half-bared and she donned a simple necklace of pearls that had come down to her from her mother. Penelope's own gown was white, with a square neck cut high enough to look demure. Whether her behaviour would be the same at her first dinner party was more than anyone could predict.

"I say, Kendall," said Sir Oliver loudly, "I've never known you to come to town this early. It's hot, it's smelly, and Parliament won't sit for two months or more." He refrained from adding that the only reason *his* family was in town was that they'd been forced to sell their country seat and retrench.

"I am aware," said Lord Kendall. He motioned with his chin down to the far end of the table where the young people had been placed in proximity to Penelope. "I have a duty to my niece to see her rigged out for the season and ready for company, and if that means braving the heat and the smell, so be it."

"Ah," said Sir Oliver, finally making head and tails of the situation. "That was a bad business with Trafford's curricle accident. Dashed sorry about Caroline."

"We all are," assured Lady Comfort.

"Thank you," said Lord Kendall, cornered into an awkward moment of painful reminiscence at what was supposed to be a light-hearted dinner party.

"I was just telling Mrs. Haverstall how much we enjoyed our time at the menagerie," broke in Mrs. Audeley, doing her best to dispel the awkwardness.

"Ah, the lions!" said Sir Oliver, rallying.

"Our girls are terrified of them," confided Lady Comfort, lowering her voice so that her offspring talking noisily farther down the table should not hear.

"Mrs. Haverstall is also terrified of them," said Mr. Haverstall with a grin, touching his wife's hand affectionately.

Mrs. Audeley smiled at them. It had been several years since she had seen Clarissa Haverstall. They had come out the same year and become bosom friends at the round of balls, and rout parties, and masquerades that they had both attended. Clarissa Haverstall *née* Loftgood had been talented in singing, a prodigy at the musicales where young debutantes were required to show off their skills. Despite her lack of marriage portion, she had attracted a coterie of suitors, and accepted a marriage proposal from Ned Haverstall, a young gentleman who had been dancing attendance on her all season. Overjoyed for her friend's happiness, Miss Trimble had returned to Upper Cross, married herself, and continued to correspond from afar.

The Haverstalls had stayed in London, firm fixtures of the metropolis. Ned was well-off, though not of the same exalted circles as the Earl of Kendall, and he and Clarissa were regarded as decent sorts, perfect for making up the numbers at any event during the season. Not having been blessed with children, Clarissa had taken an interest in Gyles, sending him illustrated books about animals, insects, and flowers.

Mrs. Audeley had been able to visit the Haverstalls on only two occasions, when she had convinced Mr. Audeley that it would be a fitting birthday present to take her to town. But her closeness with Clarissa had not cooled, and she enjoyed the pleasure of picking up conversations from several years ago as if they had just been speaking the other day.

"My dear Clarissa," said Mrs. Audeley, "You will be pleased to know that Lord Kendall tells me the older we grow, the less there is to be afraid of at the menagerie."

"'Pon my word, Kendall!" roared Sir Oliver, turning red with the wine and the merriment. "That's not very complimentary to the ladies, is it? Lady Comfort don't choose to be reminded of her age. I should be quite afraid to bring it to her attention."

"I daresay," replied Lord Kendall wickedly, "but when you have two sons in a regiment and two daughters to bring out for their season, one can't help but do the arithmetic—"

Mrs. Audeley shook her head at him, barely repressing a smile.

"—no matter how youthful Lady Comfort appears," he finished repentantly.

"Fie, Lord Kendall," said Lady Comfort, a little put out by the good-natured raillery. Her flaxen hair had just begun to lose its lustre, but the skin about her chin and neck was still as firm as creams and potions could contrive. "If we were not such *old* friends I would take affront."

"You do mean to bring Cassie out this year?" inquired Lord Kendall.

"Yes, and money has been flowing like water because of it," groaned Sir Oliver.

"Perhaps we could come to some sort of arrangement and have Penny and Cassie's coming-out ball together," said Lord Kendall. "If Lady Comfort were willing to organise the ball, I would most happily foot the bill."

"As long as the girls can tolerate sharing," said Lady Comfort, with experience born of having two daughters.

"They appear to be getting on famously," said Mrs. Haverstall. The older members of the party glanced down at the lower end of the table and saw that Penelope was waving her hands and talking animatedly while Miss Comfort and Miss Felicity Comfort laughed like their sides were hurting.

"There, you see!" said Lord Kendall as if it was all due to his own ingenuity—which, in point of fact, it was.

"Indeed," said Mrs. Audeley. "The friends that one makes during a first season are the friends that stay with you a lifetime." She smiled and pressed Mrs. Haverstall's hand. She was glad that Lord Kendall had contrived that they should be seated together.

"Right you are, Mrs. Audeley," said Sir Oliver, tipping his glass to her in salute.

"I suppose Mrs. Haverstall could tell us a great many tales about the young Mrs. Audeley," said her host, looking mischievous.

"No more than Sir Oliver could tell about a young Lord Kendall," retorted Mrs. Audeley.

"Hmm, yes," replied Lord Kendall, seemingly cognizant that swapping stories about their respective youths might not be fully to his credit. "Perhaps we should forgo those stories until the ladies have excused themselves to the drawing room." He grinned at Mrs. Audeley and lowered his voice. "You might find out more than you'd bargained for."

Chapter Eleven

Concerns

AFTER THE LADIES REMOVED to the drawing room, Lord Kendall found himself put through his paces as a host. He poured spirits for Mr. Tavinstock and Sir Oliver, recommended that Gyles Audeley quiz Mr. Heller on how to get a membership at Boodle's, and was just stepping back to the brandy decanter when Ned Haverstall approached him at the sideboard.

"What can I serve you?" Lord Kendall asked.

"Nothing, nothing," said Haverstall. He was a stocky man with broad shoulders and a short neck who might have found himself in the boxing ring had he come from a different class. "How exactly is it that you know Mrs. Audeley?" he asked, his eyes narrowing.

"We met in the country," said Lord Kendall vaguely.

"Is your estate in Derbyshire then?"

"Yorkshire."

"Ah," said Haverstall, still confused as to the connection. The counties might be neighbouring ones, but that certainly didn't make Lord Kendall and Mrs. Audeley neighbours. Lord Kendall continued to pour his brandy and refused to elaborate.

"Her decision to come to town was rather sudden, wasn't it?

Lord Kendall winced inwardly. The man was as tenacious as a bulldog! "I believe she had been planning on it for some time."

"Did you travel down together then?"

"My dear man," said Lord Kendall, "you are quite as curious as one of those Bow Street Runners. Tell me, do you suspect me of some plot against Mrs. Audeley?"

"No offence meant," said Haverstall, lifting his meaty hands in apology. "But she's a good friend of my wife's, and I'd hate to see her get mixed up in some havey-cavey business that was none of her fault."

"Duly noted," said Lord Kendall. "And now, please take a glass of brandy, for I am determined that you shall improve your opinion of me before you leave tonight and trade stories with your wife in the carriage."

Over in the drawing room, the ladies divided swiftly into groups aligned by age and interests, much as they had done at the dinner table. The Comfort girls were eager to know what sights Penelope had seen in London so far. And Lady Comfort was quite as curious as Mr. Haverstall concerning the friendship between her host and the widow from Derbyshire.

"I do not think I have seen you in London before, Mrs. Audeley."

"No, my lady. I am rarely in town. It is a treat to be able to visit this season."

"We are quite longstanding friends with Lord Kendall." Lady Comfort adjusted her shawl as she spoke. Even though the night was warm, she prided herself on displaying the Kashmir shawl that was the prized possession in her wardrobe. "Sir Oliver was up at Eton and Oxford with him. You seem great friends as well—was your husband close with Lord Kendall?"

Mrs. Audeley looked down at her lap demurely. "Oh, no, Mr. Audeley never had the pleasure of making Lord Kendall's acquaintance. Our friendship is of a more recent date."

"Mrs. Audeley lives in the north of England," said Mrs. Haverstall, intervening for her friend's sake as Lady Comfort's questions became more and more pointed, "and I understand that his lordship's country seat is in the north as well."

"Yes, but *how* did you become acquainted?" Lady Comfort could scent that something was unusual, and she would not be deterred from discovering it.

"I became acquainted with Miss Trafford first," said Mrs. Audeley slowly, "and as she is his ward, that soon led to an acquaintance with his lordship."

"Oh yes!" interjected Penelope from the seats on the other side of the room. "Mrs. Audeley was good enough to hide me in her garden from my wicked uncle when he was trying to spirit me away to London."

"Hide you from your wicked uncle!" exclaimed Lady Comfort. "Whatever can you mean?"

Mrs. Audeley berated herself inwardly. Her attempt to deflect Lady Comfort from the irregularity of the situation had led to just the crisis which she wanted to avoid. The Misses Comfort flocked behind Penelope, eager to hear a story that promised to be as scintillating as any Mrs. Radcliffe novel.

Clasping her hands in front of her, Penelope blinked her large eyes with emotion. "My guardian was determined to bring me to London, less than a year from the unfortunate demise of both my parents. Though I begged and pleaded with him to let me grieve in peace with my dear sisters at my side, he was implacable. He determined that my matchless beauty must be displayed in the metropolis so that he might marry me off and be rid of me."

"Your matchless beauty?" echoed Lady Comfort incredulously, but Penelope took no heed of the interruption.

"While we were *en route* through the rolling hills of Derbyshire, I escaped from the carriage and sought a place of shelter—"

"Erm, yes," interjected Mrs. Audeley, "Miss Trafford got out to take a walk and exercise her limbs while the carriage was stopped. She became lost in the unfamiliar countryside and ended up at my door."

"And the cunning Mrs. Audeley told me—"

"—that you should have some lemonade in the rose garden while we determined what was to be done."

It was close enough to reality that Penelope did not see the need to contradict. "So I waited in the pavilion, and when my wicked uncle arrived, Mr. Audeley rose to my defence and bade him unhand me and depart."

The Misses Comfort sighed dreamily at this statement, for Gyles Audeley had already imprinted himself on them at dinner as a romantic figure with his wavy chestnut hair and abstracted way of speaking.

"But since my uncle would not be denied and since he *is* my guardian by law, Mr. Audeley and his dear mother agreed to accompany me to the metropolis so that I might have some modicum of protection against my uncle's tyranny and so that he might not bully me into marrying where I do not choose. And that is how Mrs. Audeley came to meet my uncle!"

Lady Comfort looked from her sighing daughters to the stoic Mrs. Audeley to the perplexed Mrs. Haverstall. The only response to a story of this kind was to laugh or to scold. She chose the latter.

"What a naughty girl you are, Miss Trafford!" Lady Comfort rose from her chair. "This whole story is all quite irregular. Cassie, Felicity, I don't believe a tale of this kind is fit for your ears."

"Oh, but Mother," said the oldest girl, her hair the same thin flax as Lady Comfort's. "Just think of the horrors poor Penelope has faced!"

"Miss Trafford is clearly exaggerating her situation."

"But Mama—"

Lady Comfort raised a hand, forbidding further reply. She looked around the room. "There is no hostess for me to bid good-bye, so I will not feel obliged to do so. Cassie, Felicity, we will wait in the carriage. Mrs. Haverstall, would you be so good as to tell Sir Oliver that we are waiting for him there when the gentlemen return?"

Lady Comfort turned her face away from Mrs. Audeley and pointedly avoided any words of farewell. With a clamour of protest from her daughters, she ushered them out of the drawing room, down the hall, and out the front door.

Hands on her heart, Penelope watched them go, unsure what had just transpired to cause her new friends to abandon her so precipitately. Mrs. Audeley looked at Mrs. Haverstall sheepishly; the two exchanged a silent glance for half a moment before they both burst into spontaneous and uproarious laughter.

"Oh, oh, my dear," said Mrs. Haverstall, trying to catch her breath.

"The look on her face, Clarissa!" wailed Mrs. Audeley as she laughed so hard she began to cry.

"Well, I think it was very shabby of her to leave before Uncle Bertie has even come back from the dining room!" said Penelope, and it was at those words that the door opened and the six gentlemen descended upon the scene.

CHAPTER TWELVE

Rebuke

"'PON REP!" SAID Sir Oliver. "Where's Arabella and the girls?"

"Lady Comfort was indisposed," said Mrs. Audeley, attempting to regain her aplomb, "and she said she would wait for you in the carriage."

Puzzled, Sir Oliver made his good-byes and let himself out. Lord Kendall could see at a glance that something had gone terribly wrong. He made short work of packing Mr. Heller and Mr. Tavinstock out the door as well and frowned heavily at Mr. Haverstall until he too collected his wife and made his adieu.

Then, sending Gyles off to inspect his rosebush, he closed the double door to the drawing room and took a seat in one of the brass-studded wingback chairs that flanked the empty fireplace. Mrs. Audeley could not help feeling that he had set himself up as judge and that someone in this room was shortly to be put on trial.

"Well, Penny? Mrs. Audeley? What is this all about?"

Penelope, who was still unable to wipe the stare of bewilderment off her face, was the first to speak. "Oh, Uncle Bertie! It was all so peculiar. Lady Comfort took a pet to something I said and insisted on departing forthwith!"

Lord Kendall raised an eyebrow. "Being familiar with the mildness of your manner, I am incredulous how such a thing could have occurred."

"I'm sure I don't know what she could have taken exception to!"

"Hmm," replied her guardian, folding his arms over his chest. He turned to the other person present. "Mrs. Audeley, I rely on you to give me an exact account of the matter."

"Well," said Mrs. Audeley slowly, "I am afraid that Penelope may not realise that certain discussions are best had *en famille.*"

"For instance?"

"For instance, the little joke that we share about 'Uncle Bertie the Tyrant.' It came as quite a surprise to Lady Comfort that Penelope considers herself to be the heroine of a Gothic novel."

"Joke?" said Penelope, stamping her foot. "Why, what do you mean, Mrs. Audeley?"

"Only that it is something you may say quite safely with us who know you and know the truth, but it is too bad of you to spread such stories to Lady Comfort, for it will do the opposite of what you intended and give her a bad opinion of *you* rather than your uncle."

"Oh, it is horrible for you to take *his* side," wailed Penelope. "I was certain that you understood." At this, she began to sob pitifully, covering her face with her hands and peeping between her fingers to see what effect that should have upon her observers.

"Enough!" said Lord Kendall, raising his voice louder than either of them had ever heard it. "I will have no more of these

Drury Lane antics, Penelope. I will not have you abusing Mrs. Audeley with your wilfulness. If you are determined that I am an ogre of a guardian, then so be it. You are confined to your room until such time as you can speak with politeness and sincerity."

Appalled, Penelope flung open the doors of the drawing room, stormed through them, and then slammed them shut behind her. From the closed drawing room, they could hear the staccato of her furious feet as she fled up the staircase to her room.

Lord Kendall rose to his feet. "Mrs. Audeley," he sighed. "I must apolog—"

"Say no more," said Mrs. Audeley, rising herself.

He advanced toward her until they were no more than a chair's width apart.

"I would not for the world have your enjoyment of London jeopardised by Penny's antics."

"I do not think Penny's antics were solely the issue."

"Oh?" He looked down at her.

"Lady Comfort was very inquisitive about the nature of your...friendship with me."

He froze. "Mrs. Audeley, I hope that my behaviour has in no way given rise to—"

"Certainly not. You have been the perfect gentleman. I am certain that those who know me will think nothing of it."

"Hmm, well, I can tell your friends the Haverstalls already think me a dashed loose screw. I shouldn't be surprised if they warn you to cut all contact with me."

He looked at her anxiously, and she caught a glimpse of what must have been the boy's face behind the self-assured pose of

Lord Kendall the man. What was he afraid of? That she would wish to see the back of him for propriety's sake?

Their proximity in the closed drawing room became painfully apparent to her, and her skin began to tingle with warning. "I think we should do better to talk of this tomorrow." She stepped back and gave a little yawn. "Things always appear brighter in the morning's light."

"Yes, of course you are right," said Lord Kendall, shaking himself as if he had come to his senses. He strode over to the drawing room doors and opened them. "I'll send for your carriage immediately. And tomorrow—" He raked a hand through his hair with frustration. "It has been foolish of me to invite you here unchaperoned and expose you so much to public comment. Allow me to call upon *you* tomorrow, and I will set all of this to rights."

Chapter Thirteen

Realisation

M RS. HAVERSTALL CALLED ON Mrs. Audeley the following morning and they had a comfortable coze over a cup of tea with Lord Kendall the chief topic of conversation. "Our meeting was unexceptional in every way, Clarissa," said Mrs. Audeley when her friend quizzed her with the same questions Lady Comfort had put to her in the drawing room last night.

"Yes, my dear, but I should so hate to see you mixed up in some havey-cavey business or else unhappy with how things turn out."

"Havey-cavey business?" Mrs. Audeley repeated. Mrs. Haverstall looked down at her teacup.

"He is charming, I know, but—"

"Do you know anything to discredit him?"

"No, but I don't know anything *to* his credit either. He's all but disappeared from society in the last year—removed to Yorkshire to take care of his nieces."

"That seems very creditable in my book. And before that?"

Mrs. Haverstall took a bite of a biscuit. "Before that, he was a here-and-thereian. London, Bath, the countryside, Paris. Wherever a convivial party was to be found, there you could also find Lord Kendall."

"I did not know it was a crime to enjoy a good party." Mrs. Audeley's lips fell open into a teasing smile.

"Good heavens! It is certainly no crime. But as an outside observer, it has always seemed to me that Lord Kendall lacks the more serious nature that one might find desirable in..." She wrinkled her nose and took another bite of biscuit.

"What was that, Clarissa?" asked Mrs. Audeley brightly. "That one might find desirable in...?"

"Oh, la! You know what I was going to say. In a *husband!*"

"Goodness!" said Mrs. Audeley, "I should think one husband at a time would be enough for you."

"You goose. I mean you, of course. He's clearly smitten with you."

Mrs. Audeley brushed that suggestion away with a flourish. "I think he's very pleased to find someone to whom Penelope will listen. But I very much doubt that Lord Kendall intends to offer for *anyone* at this late date."

Mrs. Haverstall frowned. "That could also be a problem. You *are* a widow, my dear."

"What is that supposed to mean?" Mrs. Audeley adjusted the lace cap on her curls.

"Only that gentlemen sometimes believe that they can take liberties with a widow in a way they would not with a woman who has never been married."

"Oh, balderdash! Lord Kendall has given no indication of being a libertine, and he is far too cosmopolitan an aristocrat to fall for a country mouse like me. I daresay he sees me as a governess or duenna brought to his doorstep by the hand of fate—and by Miss Trafford's hijinks."

Mrs. Haverstall shook her head, rising from the sofa to take her leave. She took Mrs. Audeley's hands in hers and pressed them in farewell. "I beg you, friend, just be careful."

—— *ele* ——

That same morning Lord Kendall's composure was marred by the receipt of an unpleasant letter. Sir Oliver apologised for their precipitate departure last night, blaming it on Arabella's dashed nerves. But in it, he also stated that Kendall's idea of bringing Cassie out at the same time as Penelope Trafford wouldn't do. It wouldn't do at all. And so, Lord Kendall—who was prepared to foot the expense but was hoping to have been spared the trouble—was left with the unhappy prospect of having to organise a ball for four hundred on his own.

The letter did not end with oblique hints to Penelope's unsuitability. Lord Kendall's new friends were also dissected in detail. Sir Oliver stopped short of making his own insinuations, but he conveyed that his wife feared Mrs. Audeley might be a "fast" sort of female. In the future it would be best to leave off an invitation to the Audeleys when the Comforts were asked to dinner.

Lord Kendall boiled with fury at that last bit—more at himself than at anyone. He was five and forty years of age. He knew how the world worked. Of course, an unmarried gentleman could not be on such close footing with a pretty widow without unsavoury speculation taking place. And clearly, Lady Comfort had put the worst possible construction on their connection.

When Gyles came round to look at his rosebush, Lord Kendall quizzed him on how his mother did that morning. He learned that she was closeted with Mrs. Haverstall and became positively blue-devilled imagining what advice that lady would give her.

Gyles, oblivious to the contretemps that had occurred last night, blathered on about fertilisers and mulches. When the young man asked after Miss Trafford, Lord Kendall curtly informed him that she had not yet risen for the day. Disappointed not to catch sight of Penelope, Gyles took himself off.

Lord Kendall sat down at his desk to deal with the correspondence and bills his secretary had laid out for him but gave up after he caught himself staring off distractedly more than once. He wondered if he ought to send round an invitation for the Audeleys to join him for tea. But then he reminded himself that such a public display was what he must avoid for the sake of the lady's reputation. He had no intention of cutting his acquaintance with Mrs. Audeley, but from now on, he would be as above board as the topsails of a ship.

He leaned back in his heavy wooden chair and folded his hands behind his neck. Thunder and turf! Why could he not keep his mind from wandering like an errant schoolboy?

What was it about Mrs. Audeley that made her so endearing? She was not wildly clever—he had seen right through that charade of hiding Miss Trafford in the flower garden. She was not a stunning beauty—he had admired his share of exotic sirens and ravishing actresses, and he knew the difference between a pretty woman and a diamond of the first water. She was not even young—conventional wisdom said that a peer of the realm should look for a nubile companion like Cassandra Comfort to bear him children and continue the family line—he shivered with distaste at *that* thought.

But disregarding all that Mrs. Audeley was *not*, Lord Kendall was quite in awe of what she *was*. She was warm, she was comfortable, and her wide mouth was ever ready to fall into a smile or offer consolation or encouragement. And—if his suspicions were correct—it was an eminently kissable mouth too. He shook himself, forbidding his mind to linger too long on that last endearing quality.

The familiarity he had enjoyed with Mrs. Audeley over the last two weeks was not something he wanted to surrender. He wanted to spend every morning calling at her house, every afternoon taking her to the sights in London, and every evening escorting her to dinner. As nonsensical as it was, he felt extremely ill-used whenever the carriage came round to take her away from his house.

And yet, the rules of society dictated that he must curb this sudden inordinate desire for her company. A fifteen-minute morning call. A single set of dances at a ball. A nod, a bow, and a cool exchange about the weather. This was all of Mrs. Audeley that society was willing to afford him.

At this moment, he could fully sympathise with Penny's willingness to throw propriety to the wind. And yet, should he do so, Mrs. Audeley would be very much the loser in that scenario. He could not expose her any further than he already had to the wagging tongues of the ton.

He paced his study and tried to think of a solution. What was it that Mrs. Audeley had asked him back at Upper Cross? "Have you any female relatives in London who could help guide Penelope?"

No, he had no one who fit that bill of fare. But that did not mean he had no one who could lend an air of respectability to his bachelor household. Seizing writing paper, he sat at the desk and began to scribble furiously. Five minutes later a footman was running down the street bearing an urgent missive to Mrs. Miranda Gale of Cheapside.

Chapter Fourteen

The Chaperone

WHEN LORD KENDALL PAID a call that afternoon, instead of having an ebullient Miss Trafford on his arm, he was escorting a shrivelled octogenarian with old-fashioned skirts wide enough to hide a small pony.

"My father's late cousin's wife, Mrs. Miranda Gale," he said, making the introductions.

"Pleased to meet you," said Mrs. Audeley, dropping a curtsy.

"Eh? What's that?" asked the wrinkled woman, fumbling in her reticule and taking out an ear trumpet.

Mrs. Audeley adopted the volume of a street merchant hawking her wares. "I'm very pleased to meet you!"

"Pleased myself," said Mrs. Gale, uncrooking her back long enough to look Mrs. Audeley in the eye, nodding her chin a few times, and then sinking back into her hunched posture.

Lord Kendall manoeuvred her over to the tea table and deposited her in a chair while Mrs. Audeley poured the tea. The biscuits which Mrs. Haverstall had enjoyed earlier that day proved to be too brittle for Mrs. Gale's gums, and she soon resorted to dipping them in her hot drink.

"I hope Penelope has recovered her spirits," said Mrs. Audeley quietly as Lord Kendall slipped into a seat close beside her.

"Not yet," said Lord Kendall, "but I have high hopes that she will ring a peal over me at dinner tonight."

Mrs. Gale continued to suck on the edge of her biscuit without looking in their direction. Mrs. Audeley suspected that without her ear trumpet, she could not hear a word they were saying.

"You did not mention that your *father's cousin's wife* was in London," said Mrs. Audeley, unable to avoid smiling at the remoteness of the relation.

Lord Kendall's eyes fell to her lips, and Mrs. Audeley began to wonder if she had crumbs from the biscuits trapped in her teeth. "No," he said. "I had forgotten it until just this morning. I've invited her to stay at my townhouse."

"Oh?" Mrs. Audeley was unsure why such mundane information made her feel a little breathless.

"It can't be helped. I must have some sort of hostess to launch Penny properly. Lady Comfort has taken exception to her and refuses to help me organise the ball."

"And yet...I wonder if Mrs. Gale is equal to the task."

"Oh, she would be absolute rubbish at it," concurred Lord Kendall.

"Then why—?"

"As a chaperone. To add respectability to my establishment if perhaps *another* lady would like to assist with the arrangements."

He looked at her pleadingly. Those blue eyes, so clear and piercing, reminded her of the seashore, the one time Mr. Audeley had allowed her to take a trip to Bath.

"I've never organised anything on such a grand scale—"

"Yes, but you have excellent taste."

"You flatter me, Lord Kendall, but I—"

"—you are graciousness incarnate, Mrs. Audeley."

"Flattery again. Oh dear." Mrs. Audeley touched a hand to her temple. "I don't know how much longer I can hold out against it."

"Then, pray, do not." Capturing her other hand, Lord Kendall brought it towards him. "Will you come tomorrow to visit Mrs. Gale? And help *me* with the invitations?"

"Eh? What's that?" asked Mrs. Gale, sensing that her name had been used from across the room.

"Mrs. Audeley plans to call on you tomorrow," said his lordship loudly. He omitted to release Mrs. Audeley's hand. She felt as delicate as a China teapot with her small hand engulfed by his large one.

"I see," said Mrs. Gale. "Delightful." She dropped the rest of her biscuit into the teacup and then bent over it to peer into the depths.

Mrs. Audeley began to wonder if Mrs. Gale was, in fact, half-blind as well as half-deaf. "It seems you've made up my mind for me, Lord Kendall."

"You are too kind to hold it against me."

"Yes, well, I warn you I shall spend all my time helping Mrs. Gale adjust her shawls and put milk in her tea. I daresay you'd be better served by employing a secretary to write your correspondence."

"I shall take my chances that I can claim a few crumbs of your attention." His hand shifted position and his thumb came to rest right where her pulse was beating a violent tattoo on the inside of her wrist.

Garrick came to the door and announced that Mr. Heller and Mr. Tavinstock were here to call on Mrs. Audeley and Mr. Audeley.

Lord Kendall released his hostess' hand reluctantly and rose to assist Mrs. Gale out of the chair so they could make their adieux.

"So good to make your acquaintance," said Mrs. Audeley, rising as well and extending her hand to Mrs. Gale.

Lord Kendall's father's cousin's wife nodded and took Mrs. Audeley's outstretched hand into her wrinkled palm. "Good-bye. Come and see me sometime." She leaned in confidentially. "I'm staying in Grosvenor Square, you know. With my *rich* nephew. *Handsome* too."

"How lovely!" declared Mrs. Audeley in stentorian tones, the twinkle in her eye leaving Lord Kendall in no doubt that her amusement came at his expense. "Good-bye, Lord Kendall. Perhaps we shall see each other again soon."

"There is no *perhaps* about it, Mrs. Audeley."

And then Lord Kendall manoeuvred Mrs. Gale out the door while Mr. Heller and Mr. Tavinstock buoyantly gave their greetings, and Mrs. Audeley sent Garrick to tell Gyles that he ought to come down to the drawing room to greet the new batch of guests.

CHAPTER FIFTEEN

The Duke

"I SAY, MRS. A. You are looking dee-vine today," said Mr. Tavinstock. Mrs. Audeley had not exchanged much conversation with him at dinner, but now, in her own drawing room, she could tell right away that he was a rattle. At least, he was a pleasant, good-looking one. Mr. Heller, his companion, was currently more sober in countenance, but it was clear that he and Mr. Tavinstock both enjoyed a lark when the occasion presented itself.

"Came round to see if Audeley wants to drive out in the barouche. See the sights. Take the air. And yourself, of course, Mrs. A." Mr. Tavinstock bowed gallantly, causing his stiff coiffure to shift slightly. His straw-yellow hair had clearly only been tamed by the prolific application of pomade. "Always better to have a handsome woman on the arm when turning about in the barouche."

"That is very kind of you, Mr. Tavinstock," said Mrs. Audeley, acutely aware of her age around these young bucks who were barely older than Gyles.

"I think what Tavinstock means," said Mr. Heller, "is that like attracts like. With Mrs. Audeley in our barouche, we'll be surrounded by a bevy of beauties in no time."

Mrs. Audeley shook her head at this flummery. She was quite aware that she was a maternal figure, not a romantic one. Still, she agreed to go out in the barouche and changed into her moss green walking dress. She did look rather smart, she thought, stopping by the hall mirror to adjust her bonnet and tuck a sprig of green under the white ribbon to pull together the whole effect.

Gyles had needed a little persuading as he did not understand the social value of slowly driving past the Serpentine and hailing acquaintances as they passed, but in the end, he good-naturedly retrieved his beaver and climbed up beside Mr. Heller on the backward facing seat in the barouche.

The air was that lovely late summer haze with a vague promise of the crispness of autumn on the breeze. As soon as the barouche wheeled into Hyde Park, Mrs. Audeley discovered that Mr. Tavinstock was acquainted with anyone and everyone out to take the air. The barouche stopped to exchange greetings—and introductions—with a duchess, a viscount, several honourables, and a score of young ladies out with their mamas to learn the art of carriage flirtation before the start of the season.

Mrs. Audeley discovered that, thanks to Mr. Tavinstock's friendliness and Mr. Heller's address, her social capital was steadily increasing. Perhaps they need not rely on Lord Kendall to be their sole introduction into London society when the season began.

"Don't look now," said Mr. Heller in low tones, "but Warrenton and Digby are bearing down on us."

At this, Gyles immediately turned around and stared at the two men approaching on horseback. They slowed their mounts and reined in at the side of the barouche. "Mr. Tavinstock, Mr. Heller," said the taller of the two men, nodding at the two in the barouche. Mrs. Audeley judged him to be just shy of forty, with a firm seat in the saddle and the wide shoulders of a sporting man. He lifted his chin, indicating the two unknowns in the barouche with a question in his brown eyes.

"Mrs. Audeley," said Mr. Heller, "may I present his grace, the Duke of Warrenton. And beside him"—he indicated the shorter, rounder man—"Mr. Solomon Digby."

"Pleased to meet you both. This is my son, Mr. Gyles Audeley," said Mrs. Audeley, finishing the introductions.

Warrenton cast an appraising eye over Mrs. Audeley's bonnet and gown and then gave a little smile. His own coat was impeccably cut, which marked him out as a connoisseur of fashion. Mrs. Audeley was relieved to find that she had passed muster.

"You must be new to London, Mrs. Audeley," the duke said. "I would have remembered seeing you before."

"Yes, we are but newly arrived from Derbyshire."

"And did *Mr.* Audeley accompany you from Derbyshire?" the shorter fellow asked gruffly. Mrs. Audeley was less impressed with his manners and demeanour. His green paisley waistcoat was positively distasteful. Although he was probably of an age with the Duke of Warrenton, the years had been less kind, and his jowls drooped heavily beneath his sideburns.

"I am a widow, Mr. Digby."

"Are you now?" replied Mr. Digby, and his thick lips dropped into a leer.

"I say, your grace," said Tavinstock, inserting himself. "We've all been waiting to catch sight of the Incomparable from last season. Where has Lady Louisa been hiding herself?"

The Duke of Warrenton's eyes flashed with sudden emotion, and Mrs. Audeley saw his hands tighten on the reins of his mount. "You must be patient, Mr. Tavinstock," he said curtly. "The season hasn't even begun. I daresay you'll see my niece soon enough."

"The trick is," drawled Mr. Heller, "to see her before she's gone and engaged herself to some other fellow. I wouldn't expect a girl that pretty to last two seasons on the marriage mart."

"You're right about that," said Mr. Digby with a smug smile, polishing a quizzing glass on the prominent belly of his bright green waistcoat. Mrs. Audeley could not help thinking that a gentleman of his proportions ought to be more mindful of what colours he wore. "I'll lay you a monkey that Lady Louisa has a different surname next time you see her."

"I hope you are misinformed, Mr. Digby," said Mr. Tavinstock. "Young Audeley here has not even had the pleasure of catching a single glimpse of her. How cruel if she were to be spirited away over the summer."

"Nonsense," said the Duke of Warrenton. "No one has spirited anyone away." His tone was as clipped as the hedges at Hampton Court. "Shall we continue our ride, Digby?" The duke lifted his hand to his beaver and tipped it towards the barouche. "Charmed to have made your acquaintance, Mrs. Audeley. I shall call on you, if I may."

"Of course," said Mrs. Audeley, hoping that the duke did not intend to bring his uncouth friend Mr. Digby with him when he called. She was confused beyond measure by this last exchange about the duke's niece, but one thing was for certain: if the Incomparable from last season was no longer in the metropolis, then Penelope Trafford would have an easier time attracting suitors for this season.

CHAPTER SIXTEEN

Planning

WHEN MRS. AUDELEY CALLED on Mrs. Gale the following day at the Earl of Kendall's residence, she discovered that although the earl's cousin was at home to visitors, she was also used to taking a long nap in the heat of the day. It did not take long before Mrs. Gale was snoring comfortably on the settee. As Mrs. Gale's hands went slack with slumber, Mrs. Audeley rescued her hostess' teacup and saucer before her beverage could spill. Then, arranging Mrs. Gale's shawl about her, she would have let herself out of the drawing room had she not encountered a firm jaw and a broad set of shoulders nicely delineated in blue superfine.

"I come bringing gifts," Lord Kendall said, moving towards a small table by the window that looked out to the courtyard atrium at the rear of the townhouse. He set down a bottle of ink, a quill pen, and a blotter with sheets of stationery.

"For your new secretary?"

"Indeed." He pulled out a chair for Mrs. Audeley and seated her at the table.

She was glad that she had worn one of her new morning dresses, a square-necked gown in amber-coloured cotton with a row of flounces at the hem. "What are your secretary's quarterly wages?"

"Oh, I believe this secretary works from the goodness of her heart."

"How very generous of her," murmured Mrs. Audeley. She straightened a sheet of stationery in front of her and dipped the pen in the ink. "Where shall we begin?"

"The guest list for the ball," said Lord Kendall. He began to rattle off a list of dukes and viscounts and honourables—including Mrs. Audeley's new acquaintances the Duke of Warrenton and Solomon Digby—while Mrs. Audeley dutifully inscribed the names on the paper. "And who am I forgetting?"

Mrs. Audeley looked over the list, and her pearly white teeth caught on her lower lip in thought. Lord Kendall stared at her lip while she stared at the list. "You don't have *all* the patronesses from Almack's."

"That must be rectified." Lord Kendall instructed her to add Lady Sefton to the list. "I cannot imagine Penelope being denied vouchers, but I would not want to set anyone's back up by a careless omission."

"Then you must not forget Sir Oliver and Lady Comfort."

"I'm not exactly feeling charitable towards them at the present moment." He had told Mrs. Audeley about their refusal to host the ball together, but she did not know the half of how offensive Sir Oliver's letter had been.

"But you would not wish them to miss seeing how *superior* the entertainment at Kendall House is." Mrs. Audeley's face was the perfect picture of innocence beneath her lace cap. "I'm sure Penelope's ball will be the envy of every debutante and matchmaking mama." There was no possibility that Cassandra Comfort's ball could hold a candle to it.

"By Jove, you are quite correct. Of course, they must be on the list."

Across the room, Mrs. Gale stirred and mumbled in her sleep.

"It sounds as if Cousin Minerva agrees."

Mrs. Audeley shook her head. "It is *too* bad of you to have uprooted that poor old soul just for your own ease and comfort."

Lord Kendall lifted his hands in protest. "It is for *her* comfort. I assure you that she has been nothing but appreciative to have a holiday in Mayfair and to be squired about London by such a rich and handsome gentleman."

Mrs. Audeley laughed at that, a long musical laugh that brightened the whole room.

"What are you two plotting in here?" demanded a girlish voice.

"Ah, Penny," said Lord Kendall, gesturing for her to join them at the table. "Mrs. Audeley has been helping me construct the guest list for your coming-out ball."

At that announcement, all traces of ill-humour vanished from Penelope's face. "Oh, Uncle Bertie! Do you mean it? I am still to have a ball?" She clapped her hands ecstatically. "I felt certain that you would punish me by confining me to my room for the season with a diet of bread and water."

"Hmm, I ought to, but I'm feeling benevolent. And why are you so excited for a ball? I thought you would be all in a *quake* to be thrust into the society of your wicked uncle's acquaintances."

Penelope lifted her chin staunchly. "If Mrs. Audeley is at my side, I'm certain that I shall be the equal of it. Besides, I quite liked Mr. Heller and Mr. Tavinstock. Are all young gentlemen in London that good-natured?"

"They endeavour to make themselves amiable to pretty young heiresses."

Penelope missed the wry humour in his statement and took it as a matter of fact. She turned to Mrs. Audeley. "What can I do to help?"

Mrs. Audeley looked pensively at the long list they had constructed of peers, gentry, and London notables. "I suppose that we must next start writing out the cards for all these invitations."

Lord Kendall waved his hand dismissively. "No, no, that sounds far too tedious. I shall have Richards do it."

"And who, pray tell, is Richards?"

Lord Kendall's eyes twinkled. "My secretary, Mrs. Audeley."

"Your secretary! I daresay *he* does not work for you out of the goodness of his heart?"

"No," admitted Lord Kendall, "his quarterly wages keep him in stockings quite well."

Mrs. Audeley stood up from the table. "Well, then, if my assistance is no longer required—"

"Oh, but it is," said Lord Kendall hastily, rising to his feet as a gentleman ought. "I can assure you that Richards knows nothing at all about flowers. I was hoping that you might find time to call on Mrs. Gale tomorrow, and if there were any spare moments, then perhaps you could discuss the ballroom decorations with me." He cleared his throat. "And with Penny, I mean."

"Please do, Mrs. Audeley," said Penelope, with hands clasped and eyes shining.

Mrs. Audeley looked from one eager face to the other. "How could I refuse?"

"I was hoping you would say that," said Lord Kendall with a devilish grin.

CHAPTER SEVENTEEN

The Bonnet

A T THE AGE OF one-and-forty, one ought not to care about new bonnets, but Mrs. Audeley was sadly deficient in that respect. She had an eye for headgear and sorely wanted another new bonnet to vary the tedium of wearing her new chip bonnet with white trim. After surveying the household accounts, she determined that the trip to London had not been as dear as she'd feared—particularly since Lord Kendall had covered all the costs of travel. The bills with the modiste were smaller than anticipated and settled in full. There was perhaps a little money left in her pocketbook to purchase another bonnet.

She decided to go shopping the next morning before visiting Mrs. Gale in the afternoon. Gyles, involved in reading some botanical treatise, waved to her absent-mindedly, and she set out in the carriage by herself. She knew Cheapside had bonnets for less, but she could not resist the lure of browsing the shops on Bond Street, and so she had her coachman set her down there. The first milliner's shop she entered had styles too exaggerated for her to consider—the sort of wide brims and tall crowns that might be caricatured in the newspaper—but the second shop was more to her liking.

After trying on a few, she had almost settled on a poke bonnet covered with plum silk, when a warm voice floated over her shoulder. "A very fetching picture, Mrs. Audeley."

Mrs. Audeley turned around to find the Duke of Warrenton watching her as she stood before the mirror. Leaning against the wall of the shop, arms crossed, he looked as if had been observing her for some time.

"Oh!" said Mrs. Audeley, startled by the apparition. "I did not see you there, your grace." She fumbled with the ribbons of the poke bonnet to remove it from her head.

"Allow me," said Warrenton, moving closer. He deftly untied the silky ribbons, his rough fingers brushing the curve of her cheek as he did so.

Mrs. Audeley's eyes opened like a flower in full sunlight. She managed to stammer out a thank you and stepped backwards to put space between them. "What brings you to a milliner's shop this morning, your grace?"

"I came to purchase a bonnet for...my niece."

"Is she your ward?"

"Yes, my older brother died two years ago. The title devolved upon me, and Louisa came into my guardianship."

"How fortunate that she still has family to care for her. Do you have any children of your own?"

"Not that I am aware of," he said smoothly, "but one never knows for certain."

Mrs. Audeley blushed at the implications.

"Do you intend to buy that bonnet?" He looked at her searchingly.

"Oh, perhaps later. I do like to think on my purchases for a while before making them."

"Perhaps a closer inspection would help you make up your mind." He stepped closer and held out the bonnet for her perusal.

"No," blurted Mrs. Audeley looking everywhere but at his face. "I find that I think better when I have a little distance from the item under consideration."

He laid the bonnet down on a table. "Perhaps you would care to take a turn about Bond Street with me while you think."

"Thank you, your grace." Mrs. Audeley's head was in a whirl. She did not particularly want to parade around London on the Duke of Warrenton's arm, but he was so imposing in his snugly-fitted grey jacket that she was not entirely sure how to decline him. "I've promised the carriage to my son for the afternoon, however, so I must be getting back to Grosvenor Square."

"A pity," said Warrenton. His nostrils flared as he drank in her face. "Some other time then, Mrs. Audeley. I really must call upon you soon."

Mrs. Audeley gave a polite curtsy and darted out of the shop. As shopping trips go, this one had been very unsatisfactory. She thought wistfully of the plum poke bonnet that she had left behind and wondered if she might be able to return tomorrow and purchase it without interruption. She simply could *not* have done so with the Duke of Warrenton standing in front of her however. There was something unsettlingly predatory about the way he looked at her, and she recalled Mrs. Haverstall's warning about the way widows were viewed. Someone with whom to take liberties.

In the Duke of Warrenton's case, no doubt that was exactly his intention. But Lord Kendall was different, she was sure of it.

After all, had he not arranged the presence of Mrs. Gale just to protect her reputation?

At home, she had a small nuncheon, and she was just about to step out the door to visit Mrs. Gale when a parcel arrived. Curious, she unwrapped the brown paper and discovered the very bonnet that she had been admiring with its pleats of plum silk. A note fluttered out of the package:

With my compliments. – W

Mrs. Audeley gasped. It was daring beyond belief. A gentleman might send flowers to the lady he admired, but a bonnet? In her mind, it was only one step below jewellery.

"What is that?" asked Gyles, coming into the entrance hall to join her on the promenade to Lord Kendall's residence. "Did you purchase a bonnet for yourself?"

"No," said Mrs. Audeley shortly, her enthusiasm for the frilly creation entirely spoiled by the circumstances. "Someone sent it as a gift, but I shall not be keeping it."

Lord Kendall would have been all ears—and all questions—at that pronouncement, but Gyles merely nodded and folded his botanical periodical under his arm. He was too preoccupied to wonder who might have sent his mother a milliner's parcel and why it should be unacceptable.

Before she left the house, Mrs. Audeley gave Garrick instructions to package up the bonnet and send it back whence it had come. Hopefully, the Duke of Warrenton would be clever enough to take a hint and refrain from pursuing a widow who did not want to be pursued.

CHAPTER EIGHTEEN

The Governess

FOR THE NEXT COUPLE weeks, Mrs. Audeley was kept busy sorting out details of flowers, candles, musicians, and banquet food. Try as she might, Penelope would not be dissuaded from the theme of peacocks, and so shimmering fabrics in blue and green had been purchased for the windows and tables. She reminded Lord Kendall that an artist was needed to chalk out designs on the ballroom floor and sent him and Gyles scurrying all over London for a large enough supply of peacock feathers.

The ball was scheduled for the first week of November. The season would not be in full splendour until the spring, but Parliament was resuming early this year, and there were enough of the better sort in town—all eager for entertainment—that a ball at Kendall House was certain to be a lively affair. Richards, a narrowly built man with prematurely white hair, had become more Mrs. Audeley's secretary than Lord Kendall's, and she kept him busy with lists and letters to guests and vendors.

She had not had so much fun since organising the Yuletide celebration for all the villagers at Upper Cross ten years ago—and Mr. Audeley had disliked the event so exceedingly that it had not been repeated the following year. The luxury of limitless funds was not lost on her, and while she still strove to practise economy and preserve Lord Kendall's pocketbook, it was a heady delight to be able to order champagne and pineapples and pastries without a worry as to whether the bills could be paid.

Mrs. Audeley was engaged in securing temporary servers for the day of the event when, in the midst of the hubbub, a travelling carriage pulled up at the door of the London townhouse. "More footmen for hire?" asked Mrs. Audeley as Richards rose from his escritoire to look out the window of the earl's study.

"No, ma'am," said the wiry secretary, a portion of his professional composure dissolving into curiosity. "I believe that his lordship's nieces have arrived."

A squeal of girlish enthusiasm filtered through the study doors. "I believe that you are right."

Lord Kendall had taken Penelope and Gyles to Vauxhall that morning—after a good deal of teasing from Penelope—but he had not been able to prevail upon Mrs. Audeley to abandon her list of tasks and come with them. Mrs. Gale, however, was in the house, and Richards went to alert her about the new arrivals.

The commotion in the hall increased. Mrs. Audeley waited a few moments and then cracked open the door of the study just in time to hear Mrs. Gale's standard query: "Eh, what's that you say?"

As Mrs. Audeley opened the door fully, a profusion of dark curls, smudged pinafores and stuffed bandboxes greeted the eye. There were two girls with the same arresting blue eyes that the whole family seemed to have, but rather than Penelope's elfin countenance, their faces were broader, sweeter. One was about eight years old and the other was just a little younger than Penelope. Beside the girls stood a woman with honey coloured hair and a heart-shaped face, dressed in a drab colour of grey but unmistakably a beauty of the first order.

The older of the blue-eyed girls responded to Mrs. Gale. "I said that we're Ginny and Milly and we're here to see Uncle Bertie—unless we've come to the wrong house. Oh, goodness! What if we have?" The two girls gasped and clutched each other's hands. Mrs. Audeley could see that Penelope was not the only one given to histrionics.

"My dear girls," said the honey-haired beauty. "That is quite impossible. The driver is your uncle's own coachman and would not have deposited us at a strange abode."

"But who *are* you gels?" asked Mrs. Gale, attempting to stand upright enough to get a good look at them. Richards supported her withered arm manfully. "Never set eyes on you before."

Mrs. Audeley decided that it might be best if she intervened. She had contrived over the last couple weeks to find just the right volume that would neither exhaust her vocal cords nor be inaudible to Mrs. Gale. "My dear Mrs. Gale," she said, stepping out into the hallway, "these are his lordship's nieces."

"And you"—she turned to the voluptuous beauty—"must be their governess?"

"Yes, I am Miss Lymington." The woman dropped a brief curtsy to Mrs. Audeley.

"But who in the world are you two ladies?" asked the taller of the two girls, her blue eyes wide with confusion. "And where is our Uncle Bertie?"

"Mrs. Gale is your grandfather's cousin's wife," said Mrs. Audeley. "And I am..."

"A friend of the family," broke in a cheery voice. Without them noticing, the front door had opened again, and Lord Kendall strode into the hall with Penelope and Gyles not far behind.

"Mrs. Audeley is my guardian angel," said Penelope, releasing Gyles' arm in the joy of seeing their new visitors.

"Penny! Uncle Bertie!" The two girls ran towards the door, the elder clasping Penelope in a tight embrace and the younger jumping into Lord Kendall's arms where she was given an enthusiastic kiss on the cheek.

"Ginny, Milly, what a surprise! I did not expect you till tomorrow."

"Miss Lymington did not like the look of the first inn you had arranged," explained Ginevra. "So, we travelled on for several hours after that to find another one and got ahead of schedule."

"Did not like the look of the inn," repeated Lord Kendall, incredulously. "Pray, what was wrong with it, Miss Lymington?"

The governess folded her gloved hands and glanced down demurely. "The sheets were insufficiently aired. And the manners of the innkeeper left something to be desired."

Camilla, still in her uncle's arms, leaned in to whisper loudly in his ear. "He pinched Miss Lymington. On the bottom!"

The whole room, save Mrs. Gale, heard the whispered disclosure quite clearly. The governess turned a becoming shade of pink. Penelope gasped dramatically. Gyles—ever the knight-errant—frowned fiercely.

Lord Kendall's eyebrows flew up. "I apologise for the indignity you suffered, Miss Lymington. I can only hope that the second inn you found was more to your satisfaction."

"It was, your lordship." The governess compressed her lips firmly and gave her employer a frosty glare.

Silence fell. The tension between Miss Lymington and Lord Kendall was wound as tightly as a capstan cable.

Lord Kendall looked around the room. "Right then. Richards, I think you had better escort Mrs. Gale to her room for a rest." It was a welcome instruction as the slight Richards was nearly at the end of his strength trying to keep Mrs. Gale and her voluminous swathe of skirts upright. "Penny, could you please see the girls and Miss Lymington to their rooms and help unpack their things?"

He cleared his throat. "And Miss Lymington, perhaps you would grant me the favour of your company in my study later. I have questions about my wards' progress since last I saw them."

Miss Lymington's eyes flashed with annoyance. Clearly, she was not as demure as she pretended to be. Lord Kendall fixed his gaze on her, however, and after a few seconds, she nodded in acquiescence.

Mrs. Audeley moved towards the door. "Gyles and I will make our adieus."

"Oh, please stay!" said Lord Kendall, setting Camilla down on the floor. "We've only just got back from Vauxhall, and I daresay you would like to hear all about it."

"I only came to call on Mrs. Gale," Mrs. Audeley reminded him, "and I should not like to intrude on a family reunion."

"Your presence could never be an intrusion."

"Better to leave friends wishing for more of my company than to tire them out with it."

"Then you must call again tomorrow."

Mrs. Audeley smiled sweetly. "I have some other engagements tomorrow, but we will doubtless have you and all the girls over to dine soon." Taking hold of her son's arm, she led him out the door and down the steps.

Chapter Nineteen

Misapprehensions

"MOTHER," said Gyles reproachfully, after the heavy door had swung shut, "I had intended to look in on my rosebush before we departed."

"It will be there tomorrow."

"Why are you behaving so oddly? You've spent every day at Kendall House the last week, and now you want to leave it like the house is on fire."

The house was *not* on fire, but Mrs. Audeley was not convinced that her heart was free from flames. The carriage came round, and Mrs. Audeley let her son hand her inside before answering. "It is only polite to leave the family to themselves for some time alone."

"I suppose." Gyles fell silent. Then, in an explosive volley, he asked a question as if it had been growing so large in his mental consciousness that he could no longer keep it in. "Did you notice that governess?"

Mrs. Audeley hesitated. "Miss Lymington?"

"Yes." Gyles pursed his lips and stared up at the ceiling of the carriage. "She was very brave to travel so far with her charges without the protection of a gentleman."

"Indeed, she was." Mrs. Audeley cast her son an exasperated glance. Why must he be so susceptible to the charms of every female fate threw at him?

She could not help noticing that Lord Kendall had also seemed very sensitive to the governess' presence. But then, was it really surprising that a man in his prime should be attracted by a remarkable beauty like Miss Lymington with her statuesque figure and honey gold tresses?

"She did not look like a Yorkshire woman," Gyles mused.

"I daresay governesses can come from anywhere," said Mrs. Audeley brightly, wishing Gyles would drop this unpleasant subject.

"Perhaps I shall be properly introduced to her tomorrow."

She touched her fingers to her forehead and began to massage her temples. "Perhaps."

By the time the carriage had crossed the square and turned up the road to their townhouse, Mrs. Audeley had a headache of Jovian proportions. "If you don't mind, Gyles, I think I'll retire for the rest of the day and take a tray in my room for dinner."

"Oh? Do you have a headache?" Gyles did not think to ask what had brought it on. "I do hope you feel better after a lie down."

Mrs. Audeley smiled faintly, certain that the only thing that would alleviate her headache was knowing what exactly Lord Kendall was discussing with the voluptuous governess in the privacy of his study.

The following day, when Gyles Audeley made his daily pilgrimage to visit his rosebush, he was rewarded by an introduction to Miss Lymington. To his dismay, he discovered that although she directed her charges with a clear eye and a firm voice, she could not be prevailed upon to exchange more than three words with a gentleman.

"She's always frigidly civil like that," confided Penelope. "I think even Uncle Bertie is a little afraid of her. He insisted on leaving for London not three days after he hired her."

"No doubt she feels the need to maintain her authority as a governess and create a sense of separation," mused Gyles.

"No doubt," said Penelope with a giggle, "but she's not a bit of fun. I can't think why Ginny and Milly are so attached to her."

Lord Kendall inquired about Mrs. Audeley's health, but Gyles was sorry to report that his mother was still having a case of the megrims and was not back to her usual routine.

"Perhaps I ought to call on her?" Lord Kendall asked hopefully.

"She hasn't received anyone today other than her friend Mrs. Haverstall—and that was upstairs in her chambers since she wasn't feeling up to coming downstairs."

The light died in Lord Kendall's eyes. "The London air must not agree with her."

"I can't think why not. She has always been so fond of London in the past."

Lord Kendall grimaced. Something had killed Mrs. Audeley's enjoyment of the metropolis, and he had a nagging fear that the *something* was him. Perhaps he had pressed her too hard to help with Penny's ball. Perhaps she had overexerted herself.

After three days with no sight of Mrs. Audeley, Lord Kendall sent round a bouquet of Provence roses. The following day he paid an afternoon call in person and was rewarded by the sight of Mrs. Audeley in her drawing room, looking quite fetching in a white dotted swiss morning dress with a matching cap over her brown curls.

He took her hand and pressed it. "How are you, Mrs. Audeley?"

"Feeling much improved." She was aware from the note that came with the roses that Gyles had greatly exaggerated her poor spirits. With her recent reclusiveness, no doubt Lord Kendall thought her on death's door.

Her worries about Lord Kendall's connection to Miss Lymington had not disappeared, but the arrival of the roses had given her hope. Now, the sight of Lord Kendall after so long an absence, overcame her. She slid her hand from his grasp and leaned over the tea table to conceal the slight tremor that threatened to betray more emotion than she wished.

Fortunately, Lord Kendall was too well-mannered to press the matter further. "The replies are starting to come in for the ball," he said, lifting the tails of his trim flyaway coat to take a seat on the edge of the sofa beside her. Mrs. Audeley offered him a cup of tea. The citrus notes of the brew mingled with the rose perfume that wafted from Mrs. Audeley's brown curls and the lace fichu that added modesty to the neckline of her dress.

"Is the attendance list promising?"

"Yes, Penny's debut will be properly celebrated. Richards is keeping a list of acceptances." He looked at her with concern. "I'm afraid I overtaxed you with the preparations. Can you forgive me?"

"I was happy to be of service, but I imagine I'm no longer needed now that Miss Lymington is there to assist."

"Miss Lymington!" Lord Kendall's bright blue eyes opened wide. "What would a chit like her know about planning an event for the ton?"

"Oh," Mrs. Audeley said with surprise. "When I met her, she seemed very confident at managing things."

"Miss Lymington is certainly managing, but not, I think, in the way that is necessary for this endeavour." Lord Kendall's eyes softened. "I would never wish to exhaust you, but if you would enjoy it, we could use your expertise to finish the last details of the evening."

Mrs. Audeley smiled tentatively. "I suppose it is a compliment to be wanted."

"Yes, and I have it on good authority that Richards is quite distracted with worry about your illness. You've made his job far too easy this last fortnight."

"Well, if only to set Mr. Richards' mind at ease—"

"Thank you. You are an angel of mercy, Mrs. Audeley." Lord Kendall took her hand and pressed it to his lips. Mrs. Audeley felt a tingle of pleasure course through her. It was only gratitude, of course, but she enjoyed the feeling of being needed.

When Lord Kendall omitted to release her hand, she drew it away slowly. His bright blue eyes continued to play over her face as if he had left something still unsaid.

"What are you thinking about?" she asked abruptly.

Lord Kendall straightened and grinned. "I'm thinking that all work and no play makes Bertie a dull boy. What do you say to a night at the theatre to celebrate your recovery?"

CHAPTER TWENTY

Secrets

R EASSURED OF THE EARL'S need for her assistance, Mrs.
Audeley resumed her calls on Mrs. Gale, each of which
inevitably ended in a protracted conference or comfortable coze
with Lord Kendall. The upcoming ball dominated the majority
of their conversation and calendar, but there was also time to
entertain Penny, Ginny, and Milly with outings to Hatchard's
book shop or walks in Green Park.

On one occasion, when Lord Kendall had taken Gyles down
to Angelo's to watch a bout of fencing, Mrs. Audeley invited
Penny, Ginny, and Milly to accompany her on a shopping expedition. Mrs. Gale was indisposed, but the girls, along with Miss
Lymington, crowded into the carriage and set off for Pall Mall.

Mrs. Audeley noticed that Miss Lymington's brown eyes
were bright and alert in the carriage, but as soon as they dis-
embarked onto the pavement, she bowed her head and bent her
shoulders so that her face was obscured by her bonnet and her
whole person was hardly recognizable. It seemed incredible that

a young woman as forceful as this governess should be shy of being in public.

When they reached Pall Mall, Penelope's eyes were immediately drawn to the windows of Harding Howell & Co. The ladies stepped inside and found themselves in an enchanted forest of furs, fans, silks, muslins, lace, and gloves.

"I must have these," declared Penelope, drawing a pair of long rose-coloured silk gloves over her slender fingers.

"I do think *white* gloves would be more the thing," murmured Mrs. Audeley.

"Yes, they are certainly more common, but I shall be *noticed* with these."

"Attracting notice is not always for the best," said Miss Lymington. She tried to shepherd the girls away from the gloves table and over to the ormolu clocks in the next section of the store.

"That's right," parroted Camilla. "You don't want to look like a bit o' muslin."

"Milly," said Mrs. Audeley, looking at the eight-year-old with dismay, "wherever did you learn such language?"

"Mother used to say it," said Ginevra. "That there was always some bit o' muslin chasing after Uncle Bertie, which is why he could never stay put in one place."

Miss Lymington looked up sharply. "A young lady does not mention such things, Ginny. And besides, your uncle rates his charms far too highly."

"I believe that was Mrs. Trafford's assessment of the situation, not Lord Kendall's," said Mrs. Audeley, annoyed by the governess' tone. It was entirely plausible that over the last two decades scores of women, suitable or not, had thrown themselves in Lord Kendall's path. Or inveigled their way into being his dinner partner. Or fainted into his strong arms in the ballroom. It would be strange if women had *not* noticed him.

A soft blush came over her cheeks as she shepherded her wayward thoughts and turned back to Ginevra. "Lord Kendall is perfectly able to stay put in one place when his responsibilities demand it. Didn't he keep you company in Yorkshire all last year?"

"Yes, until Miss Lymington arrived," said Penelope with a look of perfect innocence on her face. She had drawn both rose-coloured gloves over her arms now and was admiring them in the mirror. "And then, for some reason, he felt compelled to leave for London. So, perhaps Mother was right after all about why Uncle Bertie is such a here-and-thereian."

The governess shot Penelope a look of pure disdain. "I should warn you, Miss Trafford, that you will never be considered an Incomparable with such outlandish taste."

"But at least I will also never be a governess."

"Girls," said Mrs. Audeley, gaining their attention more by the intensity of her tone than the volume of it. "We will not speak so to each other."

"Yes, Mrs. Audeley," said Penelope, dutifully chastened. But the fire in Miss Lymington's eyes did not abate.

The three sisters entered the perfumery section of the shop and began to try the shop assistant's patience by testing every fragrance available, but Miss Lymington hung back in the corner with Mrs. Audeley.

"You are very young to be a governess."

"How old do you think I am?"

"I should be surprised if you were more than one-and-twenty."

Miss Lymington did not reply to that, but her full lips compressed into a thin line. Mrs. Audeley could see that she had guessed rightly. The cloying sweetness of the blended perfumes began to give her a headache, but she pressed on with her questioning.

"How did you gain the position teaching the Misses Trafford?"

"I answered an advertisement Lord Kendall had placed and took the post to Yorkshire."

"And yet, you do not seem to have been born a governess or even to be enthusiastic about the position. Had you no other options?"

"No, Mrs. Audeley." Her clipped tone and turned shoulders ended the conversation.

As they waited for the young ladies to finish their experimentation with the fragrances, Mrs. Audeley reflected that despite all of Miss Lymington's arrogance, she seemed like a wild animal trapped in a cage, ready to claw at anyone who came near no matter if they were friend or foe. If matters had been different, perhaps she and Penelope could have been friends. But as things were, there was some difficulty clouding Miss Lymington's brow and some mystery clouding her past.

CHAPTER TWENTY-ONE

Fencing

LORD KENDALL SOON DISCOVERED that Gyles Audeley did not know the first thing about fencing. They were watching a bout with two equally matched gentlemen at Angelo's *Ecole des Armes* on Bond Street. One of them was Mr. Heller. Lord Kendall hoped that Gyles would at least be interested in the outcome of the match. "I take it your father was not much addicted to sport?"

"No, not at all. He rode out with the hounds when he had to, but he did not enjoy it."

"A bookish man then?" said Lord Kendall, attempting to find the lay of the land. He sipped a coffee while they sat at a small table on the outskirts of the fencing floor.

"No," said Gyles, a curious look coming into his eyes. "I would not say that either. I think I can count on one hand the times I saw him open a book to read."

"Then what were his passions?"

Gyles hesitated. "Money, I suppose. The managing of it. He did not have a great deal of it, but what he did have, he tended and cultivated as carefully as I would a rosebush."

The room exploded into a general uproar, and Lord Kendall began to clap. "A good hit." The Viscount Landsdowne had pricked Mr. Heller with the tip of his foil on the ball of the right shoulder. Undaunted, his opponent motioned to continue, and the room settled down again to watch.

"Was he generous?"

"With me, yes."

"But not with others, one could infer."

Gyles sighed. "He was not particularly generous with my mother, especially later, when it was apparent she could not—" He waved his hand vaguely. "You know what I mean."

"No, I'm at a loss."

Gyles blushed. "Infants. Babies. I was the only one she could bring to term."

"Ah." Lord Kendall's response was short and measured. "Naturally a woman's worth should be predicated on the number of children she can bear."

"I'm afraid I don't subscribe to that idea, my lord." Gyles' dreamy eyes focused, and his lips set into a firm line.

"So, you wouldn't plough down a rosebush that didn't bloom and plant another?"

"A woman is not a rosebush."

"Indeed," said Lord Kendall softly. It was clear that the young man was cut from a different cloth than his father had been.

As they talked, Solomon Digby, an old, fat fellow with a bright mauve waistcoat, entered the salon and took up a position near their table. "Careful, Digby," said the earl. "You're blocking our view of the match."

"Oh, pardon me," said Mr. Digby, taking off his beaver and scratching his balding head. "Hello, Kendall. Audeley."

"I'm surprised to see you here," said Lord Kendall. "Angelo's is hardly your typical tea and biscuits." Indeed, it was common knowledge that Solomon Digby was frequently found at the haunts of vice in London, in the early hours of the morning with wine, women, and song upon his lips.

"You're right of course," said Mr. Digby. "But I need some information. There's a gel promised to me, but her guardian keeps putting me off. Haven't seen hide nor hair of her since midsummer. Where's she got to, I'm wondering? Thought I'd get to a watering spot and hear the latest gossip."

"You speak as if this girl were a horse," said Gyles, perplexed.

"Oh, stap me, certainly not," said Digby, contradicting himself in the next breath. "This one's a prime filly, high-mettled, not quite broken to harness."

"Does this filly have a name?" inquired Lord Kendall.

Digby looked to the right and to the left and then leaned in confidentially. "It's Lady Louisa, Warrenton's niece."

"An heiress, I believe."

Digby's jowls jiggled as he nodded. "On her mother's side. A hundred thousand pounds."

"No wonder you're looking for her," said Lord Kendall dryly.

"Oh, she has other qualities as well," said Digby hastily, and he launched into some anatomical details that soon had Gyles' ears flaming red with embarrassment.

"And so Warrenton's putting you off, is he?" asked Lord Kendall, displaying a keen interest in the imbroglio. "What does he say?"

"He says she's visiting family in a remote location. Claims she'll be back in London at the start of the season."

"Why, then you must just be patient, man," said the earl, slapping Mr. Digby on the back. "If you trust Warrenton, that is." That last thought was tossed out casually, grist for the mill of thought should Mr. Digby be inclined to engage the wheels of his mind. Digby frowned and sauntered on to the next group of Corinthians.

The room erupted again as the viscount landed another good hit. Lord Kendall rose from his chair to applaud.

"The winner!" said Henry Angelo, the fencing master. He lifted Viscount Landsdowne's arm in the air. The fair-haired young man smiled in exhaustion, still breathing heavily from the bout while his opponent, Mr. Heller, attempted to paste on a pleasant face about the loss. Kendall moved onto the fencing floor to congratulate the viscount. "Good show, Landsdowne."

"Thank you," said the viscount, who was mopping his face with a towel. "I thought Heller had me cornered a minute ago. It was a miracle I managed to parry."

"Parry and riposte. It was elegantly done. Tell me," said the earl smoothly, "did you get my card for the ball at Kendall House?"

"Ah, yes, I suppose I did," said the viscount. "I probably ought to have my secretary reply to that."

"In the affirmative, I hope."

"Yes, I'll be there."

"Good, because there's something I was hoping you would do for me. The ball's in my niece's honour, you know...."

And with that preamble, the earl took Lord Landsdowne aside and explained the favour needed while Gyles went to exchange a few words with the humbled Mr. Heller.

CHAPTER TWENTY-TWO

The Theatre

LORD KENDALL HAD ENGAGED a box at the Royal
Opera House in Covent Garden, and the Audeleys
agreed to accompany him and Penelope to the theatre the
week before the ball. Ginny and Milly begged to come along,
stating that they would be sure to behave with their governess to chaperone, but Miss Lymington insisted that it was
not at all appropriate for young ladies. There would be time
enough for plays and operas when they had *their* season in
London.

Mrs. Audeley planned to wear the chocolate silk evening
dress. It had seen extensive use in the last month, and she
tried to stuff down a niggling sense of discontent. She could
pretend she had enough funds to order a second evening
dress, but it would seriously deplete their finances for the
rest of the season. As it was, she decided she would change
the look of the dress by adding some cream lace around the
neckline and putting a feathered bandeau in her hair.

Penelope, who had chosen a gown of pale pink ruffles, inveigled Lord Kendall into letting her wear the Trafford diamonds—although he drew the line at allowing the necklace, earbobs, *and* bracelet. "A debutante dripping with jewels is not quite the thing. Pick *one*, Penny."

That afternoon, when the safe in Lord Kendall's study was opened to obtain the jewels which had belonged to the girls' mother, Penelope gasped and sighed at each string of sparkling stones. "Oh, Uncle Bertie! How exquisite. Surely, you would much rather have me display these than keep them all locked up in the dark."

Ginevra, who was more moderate in her excitement, was also more discerning with her taste. "Those emeralds are far too large for you, Penny. But look, these garnets would complement Mrs. Audeley's complexion quite nicely."

"Oh, yes, they would!" cried Penelope, rapturously holding them up to Mrs. Audeley's neck. "My dear Mrs. Audeley, you must borrow them for the theatre tonight."

"Dear me, no," said Mrs. Audeley quickly. She had never worn anything finer than her pearls, and the size and cut of the garnet necklace quite intimidated her. Remarkably, however, Lord Kendall added his voice to the chorus of Penny and Ginny, and she finally capitulated and agreed to wear the garnet necklace.

When she left Kendall House and returned home to dress for the evening, she nearly had second thoughts about the garnets. But a closer look in the mirror revealed that the deep red and old gold matched her skin perfectly. She decided to forgo the cream lace and placed some deep red rosebuds in her hair instead. Gyles, oblivious to the necklace, complimented her on the flowers, and Mrs. Audeley was soothed into believing that her appearance was entirely sedate and unremarkable for a widow who meant to blend in to her surroundings.

They arrived shortly before the curtain rose that evening, for Penelope had strenuously objected to being late. She had not yet mastered the feigned boredom of fashionable society and still wanted to see everything there was to see. The *hoi polloi* who filled the floor of the theatre were just as eager, but Lord Kendall squired his party masterfully through the throngs in the corridors. With Gyles' help, he nearly carried Mrs. Gale up the staircase that led to their box, and once she was settled in a chair in the corner, the octogenarian promptly fell asleep.

"You are fortunate we were not in London last autumn," Lord Kendall said to his three companions as they gazed breathlessly around the interior of the opera house. "The new theatre had just opened after a fire destroyed the old one, and there were riots every night during the performance."

"Riots?" asked Mrs. Audeley. "Whatever for?"

"Yes, why?" demanded Penelope. "I would think people would be *happy* to have the theatre back."

"The prices were increased by one shilling a ticket. Londoners do not take kindly to an assault on their ancient rights and privileges."

"All that over a paltry shilling!" scoffed Penelope.

"It seems that the crowds have adjusted to the new prices by now," said Gyles. He nodded at the full boxes and packed floor of the gilded room.

"Oh no," said Lord Kendall, his eyes twinkling. "The proprietor was forced to lower the prices to halt the riots. Only then was civility restored, and thankfully, we can all enjoy the theatre again."

"Will we see Sarah Siddons tonight?" asked Penelope, her wide blue eyes flitting from the red velvet curtains to the gilded chandeliers, to the domed roof. The din that filled the room was louder than anything she had ever experienced—although it did not seem to disturb Mrs. Gale in the corner.

"But of course. She plays Lady Macbeth tonight, and her brother Macbeth himself."

Lord Kendall gave Penelope and Gyles the seats closest to the stage while he and Mrs. Audeley sat comfortably behind them, for the box could seat at least eight. Gyles offered Penelope his newly-purchased opera glasses so that she could take in the details of the stage more fully, and she began to peer around the room like a bird watcher on the moor.

"I must confess," said Mrs. Audeley, "that I have never seen this play before." She cast a veiled glance at Lord Kendall. "I daresay you think me woefully provincial."

"Not so. I merely envy you the treat of experiencing the story for the first time." He leaned closer to murmur in her ear. "You must let me know if you have trouble following it, and I will explain it to you."

"Look!" said Penelope, peering through the opera glasses at a box across the theatre. "There is Lady Comfort and Cassie with her." Penelope waved enthusiastically and was gratified to see Miss Comfort return the salutation until her mother's gloved hand arrested the gesture.

"Thunder and turf," said Lord Kendall quietly. "Now I'll have to stop Penny from dashing over there at the intermission. I wouldn't put it past Lady Comfort to give her the cut direct."

"Surely she would not be so cruel."

Lord Kendall frowned. "When Arabella sets her back up, there's no reasoning with her."

"You speak as if from experience."

"Yes," said Lord Kendall. "Painful experience. I happened to displease her once and it was years before Sir Oliver was allowed to fraternise with me again."

"The curtain!" shrieked Penelope. "It's starting!"

Mrs. Audeley looked to the stage and was instantly transported by the costumes and pageantry. Immersed in the soliloquies, the witches, the ghosts, the guilt, she leaned forward in her chair, lips slightly parted, eyes wide. Throughout it all, she failed to notice that Lord Kendall was so bored with the performance that he spent the entire first act watching his neighbour intently, appreciating every intake of breath, every shiver of excitement, every glitter of garnets, and every shimmer of chocolate silk in the candlelit confines of the Theatre Royal.

CHAPTER TWENTY-THREE

Drama

A T THE INTERMISSION, LORD Kendall's predictions were proved correct, and Penelope inveigled Gyles into taking her around the theatre to converse with Cassandra Comfort. "I'd best go too to mitigate the damage," said Lord Kendall apologetically. "Shall you be all right here by yourself?"

"You forget that I have Mrs. Gale," said Mrs. Audeley, casting a glance at the snoring chaperone in the corner. "I shall be quite all right here." Mrs. Audeley had the good sense to realise that Lady Comfort would have far more patience with Penelope if the undesirable Derbyshire widow was nowhere to be seen.

The round theatre was as lively as a beehive. Mrs. Audeley leaned over the seat to retrieve Gyles' opera glasses and amused herself by watching the antics of the humbler folk in the floor seats, jostling and jesting as they waited for the intermission to end. Lifting her line of sight, she peered at aristocrats and gentry posturing and posing in their theatre boxes. Looking at the Comforts' box, she was pleased to see that Lady Comfort had received Miss Trafford without incident and that Penelope was talking animatedly to Cassie while Gyles formed a handsome backdrop.

There was another woman in the box with them who had the look of Lady Comfort about her but had the misfortune to not have kept her figure so well and looked quite portly in her green evening gown. Mrs. Audeley wondered if it were a cousin or perhaps a sister, and she also wondered where Lord Kendall had disappeared to, for her opera glasses told her that he had not entered the Comfort box alongside his niece.

She was so engaged in speculation that she failed to notice her own box had been invaded. A stranger loomed behind her half-bare shoulder and laid a gloved hand upon it. She jumped in her seat. "Oh, your grace! You startled me."

"Good evening, Mrs. Audeley." The Duke of Warrenton circled around to the seat that Lord Kendall had recently occupied, lifted the black coattails of his evening jacket, and sat down as if he meant to stay for a while. "How are you enjoying the performance?"

Mrs. Audeley felt her fingers tighten around the opera glasses as they lay in her lap. "It is very convincing, especially Lady Macbeth." She was surrounded by hundreds of people above and below her and Mrs. Gale's wrinkled chin was rising and falling against her collar not ten feet away. And yet, she felt far too vulnerable in the red-curtained box. The only safety was in keeping the conversation flowing. "I'm sure you must have seen Sarah Siddons before?"

The duke inclined his head in acknowledgment. "But one doesn't go to the theatre to see the actors, but rather the audience." He angled his body towards Mrs. Audeley. "I was disappointed you sent back that bonnet, but the sight of you at the theatre tonight has illuminated the situation."

"It has?" Mrs. Audeley's lips parted with surprise.

"Of course." He leaned closer and examined the cut surface of the garnet necklace arrayed around her collarbone. "I can tell that you are the sort who would only accept gifts from one gentleman at a time, and I suppose you're right to choose Kendall. I may be a duke and he an earl, but he's far plumper in the pocket than I. However, you ought to know that I will be coming into a tidy fortune very soon. So, when you tire of Kendall, let me know. I will be waiting in the wings."

Mrs. Audeley flushed pink from the tips of her ears to the top of her collarbone. What was he insinuating? Surely, he could not mean—

"Warrenton," said a steely voice from the curtain to the rear. "I don't believe I invited you into my box."

"Oh, there you are Kendall." The duke rose from his seat and gave an affected yawn. "Since we're old friends, I did not think to stand on ceremony."

"I did not realise you were acquainted with Mrs. Audeley."

"We were introduced at the park a few weeks ago," said Mrs. Audeley, determined to make their acquaintance as innocuous as possible.

"Hmm," said Lord Kendall. "One of the disadvantages of the fresh air. It leaves one open to company of all sorts."

"How cross you are tonight," said Warrenton. "And how ungentlemanly of you to leave your lady friend unattended." His eyes flicked scornfully to the sleeping Mrs. Gale and back again. "If I had such a lovely lady on my arm, I would be more solicitous for her comfort."

"Oh?" Lord Kendall's eyebrows rose to a magnificent height. "I have not seen Lady Louisa on your arm lately. Is *she* all alone in your theatre box?"

The Duke of Warrenton frowned, and Mrs. Audeley noted that the set of his chin was truly forbidding. "My niece is not in London at present."

"How disappointing. Where is she? Bath?"

"That is none of your concern."

The duke moved towards the curtain at the rear of the theatre box, but Lord Kendall was not done needling him. "Rumour has it that she's disappeared entirely. You'd better produce her soon, Warrenton, if you want to scotch the stories people are telling."

"Mind your own business, Kendall."

"But it's too enticing to mind yours for you. Tell me, who gets the inheritance if Lady Louisa dies? You?"

"What a commonplace mind you have, Kendall," said the duke stiffly. "I may be a rogue, but I'm not a murderer."

"Ah, then you must have some other reason for hiding Lady Louisa away from us."

Attempting to control his pique, the Duke of Warrenton gave a courtly bow to the object of his interest. "Your servant, Mrs. Audeley." And then, without even a nod to the earl, he turned on his heel and exited the theatre box.

Laughing at the duke's discomfiture, Lord Kendall resumed his seat, but the laugh swiftly disappeared from his face when he saw how distressed Mrs. Audeley appeared. "What is it? Has Warrenton upset you?" His bright blue eyes flickered with concern.

"No, no," said Mrs. Audeley. Her eyes darted around the gilded theatre at the hundreds of raucous Londoners enjoying the intermission and at the scores of eyes glancing off her theatre box like tennis balls. Had every mind in this sea of people jumped to the same conclusion as the Duke of Warrenton? "Tell me, Lord Kendall, do these garnets actually belong to Penelope?"

Lord Kendall hesitated. "No, Mrs. Audeley. They were my mother's."

"So, I am wearing your jewellery?"

"In a matter of speaking." He sent her an apologetic glance. "But Penelope was so adamant, I forgot to mention it. Do you mind?"

Mrs. Audeley felt red unfurl like petals across her cheeks. "I am afraid someone might recognize them and expose us both to public comment."

"The catalogue of the Kendall family jewels is not widely known, and my mother has been dead these ten years or more. The garnets have been imprisoned in my safe for a decade. It seemed a remote possibility that anyone would recognize them."

Mrs. Audeley smiled faintly, "I'm sure you're right." But as Gyles and Penelope returned to the box and the second act resumed, Mrs. Audeley could not suppress the feeling that the Duke of Warrenton had known exactly *whose* necklace she was wearing. If any other theatre-goers were just as observant, she could only hope that they were not drawing the same conclusions as he had.

CHAPTER TWENTY-FOUR

The Ball

T HE REST OF THE preparations for the ball went off with only minor setbacks. The hothouse lilies that were supposed to arrive the day before the ball failed to materialise, but thankfully, Mrs. Audeley had the good sense to send Gyles to Sir Abraham Hume for help, and he assisted them in obtaining dozens of white roses in lieu of the lilies.

"They are not as exotic as I like," said Penelope, comparing the unfurling petals to the opulence of the peacock feathers in the arrangement.

"Ah, but sometimes a simple country rose is the perfect foil for flamboyance," said Lord Kendall. He cast a curious look at Mrs. Audeley as he said this, but she was too occupied to consider what he might mean.

"Let me help with the flowers," begged Camilla, but Mrs. Audeley was clever enough to find another task for her and sent her to the kitchen to count the miniature fruit tarts that Cook had made to ensure there were enough.

It was late afternoon by the time all of the last-minute details had been sorted to Mrs. Audeley's satisfaction. Lord Kendall implored her to go home and rest so that she would be ready to dance that evening. "Yes, yes," she said as he was urging her out the door, "but you must make sure that the maids set out more candles in the card room, and they cannot forget the ice for the punch to be put in at just eight o'clock."

"Go home, Mrs. Audeley," insisted Lord Kendall, "and if you are not too run off your feet, I will make bold to claim the supper dance with you. Then you can sit at table and whisper in my ear everything that has gone wrong with the white soup and the negus, and I can assure you that no one else has noticed a thing."

"Very well," said Mrs. Audeley, reluctant to give up the tiller of this ship until it was truly out of the harbour. "I shall see you just after eight o'clock then."

"I shall be counting the minutes." He took her hand and brought the knuckles up to his lips and kissed them lightly. His eyes lingered on her harried face affectionately.

Back at her rented townhouse, Mrs. Audeley rested for an hour before beginning her toilette. The burgundy silk she had ordered from the modiste draped becomingly over her figure, and she pinned up her curls in a more elaborate hairstyle than usual. She had learned her lesson from the garnets at the theatre and strongly refused any of the jewellery Penelope had offered earlier that day. Instead, she promised herself the satisfaction of seeing all her labours come to fruition—while silently pretending to be a disinterested spectator at the event.

In the carriage, on the way to Kendall House, Gyles lay back morosely against the squabs. His slightly dishevelled curls and brooding countenance gave him the air of a poet, while his years of labour in the garden gave him the wiry strength of a Corinthian. Mrs. Audeley reflected that although this was Penelope's coming-out ball, it was also Gyles' first significant social appearance in London. Perhaps he would meet someone more suited to him than Penelope at the ball—since that boyish infatuation seemed to have faded.

As they came in sight of bright torches lining the entrance to Kendall House, Gyles' moody countenance finally erupted into words. "Miss Lymington is not attending the ball. She says it's her duty to stay upstairs with Ginny and Milly."

"Very noble of her," said Mrs. Audeley. Inside, she wondered just how noble it was for a young woman to simply do the job that she had been employed to do, but she kept that thought to herself.

"But it's unfair," complained Gyles. "She's far too young to be sequestered away in some attic corner when all the other young ladies are wearing out their dancing slippers. She deserves to have some fun as well."

Mrs. Audeley murmured that she did not imagine Lord Kendall's governess resided in the corner of an attic, but Gyles was too perturbed to take notice.

Finally, the moment came to disembark. Mrs. Audeley felt Gyles hand her down from the carriage step, but her eyes were riveted to the Palladian face of Kendall House. She noted with satisfaction that the liveries for the extra footmen had all been tailored to fit correctly, a last-minute task which she had assigned to Richards yesterday.

Lord Kendall and Penelope were stationed inside the door in a receiving line, while Mrs. Gale sat in a chair to their left. "Welcome, Mrs. Audeley," said Lord Kendall, taking her gloved hand in his and pressing it. "So pleased you could join us for this little event." His blue eyes glittered like gemstones, and she saw him admiring her figure wrapped in the burgundy silk.

"I wouldn't miss it, your lordship. They say it will be the event of the season."

Lord Kendall exchanged a private smile with her, and she noticed how charming were the crinkles around his eyes. "If so, I can take no credit for it. My secretary made all the arrangements."

"Oh, Mrs. Audeley!" said Penelope, hands clasped to the bosom of her pale pink ball gown. "I am to lead out the first dance, and with a viscount! I am all a-quiver with dread."

"You will be magnificent," said Mrs. Audeley soothingly. "Just follow the lead of the gentleman and try not to argue with him. At least, until the dance is over."

"Sound advice," said Lord Kendall. "I always say arguments are best saved for later." He smiled and turned reluctantly to the next guest while Mrs. Audeley waited for Gyles to give a perfunctory compliment to Penelope and then made her way into the ballroom on his arm.

Shortly afterwards, Mrs. Audeley watched as Penelope performed the opening dance with flawless steps. The Viscount Landsdowne's fair hair contrasted charmingly with Penelope's black curls, and the room was full of compliments for the new debutante. Mrs. Audeley wondered how Lord Kendall had arranged for a peer to partner Penelope but then remembered how extensive the earl's acquaintance was. Her one season in London was but a fraction of his own experience there. He was as much a fixture of the ton as Lady Jersey or Beau Brummel while she was a simple Derbyshire widow, woefully out of her depth in this crowd of sophisticates.

The Haverstalls arrived soon, and Mrs. Audeley gratefully rushed to greet Clarissa and press her hand. Here, at least, was one person she knew and could depend on. "What a glorious gown!" said Mrs. Haverstall, admiring the burgundy silk. "You look far too young to have a grown son, my dear."

"Appearances can be deceiving," said Mrs. Audeley good-naturedly. "If I were to dance every set like these young people, I should be as stiff as an old grandmother tomorrow."

Together, they watched the second set form, and Mrs. Audeley was happy to see that Gyles had secured the dance with Penelope. By now, she was well aware that the two did not suit, but she had developed affection for the motherless girl and was glad to see Gyles attending to her comfort. Lord Kendall was nowhere to be seen, and Mrs. Audeley could only assume that he was still playing host at the entrance of the house.

Halfway through the second set, Mrs. Audeley noticed that the Duke of Warrenton had entered the ballroom, accompanied by his leering friend from the park, Mr. Solomon Digby. Warrenton's eyes met hers as soon as he appeared, and he advanced towards her as if drawn by an invisible string.

The man had an imposing presence, his broad shoulders straining at the seams of his dark coat, but somehow it made Mrs. Audeley feel uneasy rather than protected. After she presented him to Mr. and Mrs. Haverstall, the duke made his reason for approach quite plain. "Mrs. Audeley, I am surprised to find you sitting out. I must claim you for the next dance."

Mrs. Audeley felt her tongue tie into knots, and she could find no reasonable excuse for refusal. "Thank you, your grace."

Once out on the ballroom floor for the cotillion, Mrs. Audeley relaxed among the rhythmic pattern of circles and turns. The duke said little although his brown eyes were fully alive.

As the neighbouring couples began their footwork, he leaned in to murmur above the music. "Your neck is deliciously bare tonight, Mrs. Audeley. Dare I hope that you have grown tired of those garnets and given their giver his *congé?*"

Mrs. Audeley swallowed and tried to still the indignant swelling of her bosom. "Your grace, I believe I must correct a misimpression you have formed. I am not used to the profligacy of town ways and am not at all interested in forming the kind of connection you seem to be hinting at."

"How curious. I had thought you a merry widow, Mrs. Audeley. Are you prepared to turn village parson on me?"

"If I must. Anything to convince you that I want no gentlemen 'friends' to occupy my time in London."

"I see. Is that why Kendall keeps glaring daggers in my direction?"

The dance drew them apart for several measures. Mrs. Audeley tried to keep her composure, taking deep breaths as she moved in time with the music. A quick scan of the ballroom revealed that Lord Kendall was indeed in the margins, watching her intently.

There were other faces attending vigilantly as well. Lady Comfort's eyes narrowed over the top of her fan as she sat in the corner waiting for her own daughter to be asked onto the floor.

"I've done nothing wrong in dancing with Warrenton," Mrs. Audeley reminded herself. But before she could put Lady Comfort out of her thoughts, the duke took her right hand in his and pulled her far closer than the dance demanded.

"I find your plain-speaking most alluring, Mrs. Audeley. It's one of the many attractions a widow presents—the opportunity to state clearly what one wants without offending maidenly sensibilities."

"Don't you mean the opportunity to gratify your desires without incurring any responsibility?"

"*Touché,* Mrs. Audeley. I suppose I do."

Although he admitted a hit, the duke's face was anything but repentant. As the music came to a close, he returned Mrs. Audeley to the outskirts of the ballroom but seemed loath to let go her gloved hand. "I do not think we have explored your objections as thoroughly as they deserve. May I claim the next dance as well?"

"Thank you, your grace," said Mrs. Audeley, withdrawing her hand and dropping an exaggerated curtsy, "but the next dance is promised to Lord Kendall."

CHAPTER TWENTY-FIVE

Venom

L ORD KENDALL BORE DOWN on the Duke of Warrenton like a ship of the line and claimed Mrs. Audeley as his prize. The next dance was a reel and left little opportunity to converse, but as she spun the reel down the line of dancers, arm in arm with Lord Kendall, Mrs. Audeley discovered that she had never enjoyed a dance half so well. At the end of the set, breathless and grinning, Lord Kendall caught hold of Mrs. Audeley's gloved elbow and began to direct her towards the dining room. "Well?" he asked with raised eyebrows.

"Well, what, your lordship?"

"What did Warrenton want?" he asked, drawing out a chair for Mrs. Audeley to the right of his own seat at the head of the table.

"Nothing worth mentioning," said Mrs. Audeley, shaking off Warrenton's insinuations like a cloud of gnats. "But I suppose now is the moment of truth."

"Truth?" Lord Kendall's face grew serious.

It was Mrs. Audeley's turn to grin. "The white soup. We must see if the recipe I so painstakingly convinced your cook to use passes muster with this crowd of hungry dancers." She looked down the long table and saw the red-cheeked partygoers lift spoon to mouth and sip the creamy broth.

Lord Kendall eyed the crowd. "Penelope is on her third spoonful, so I would call that a success."

"You cannot imagine what a relief that is to my mind."

"I rather think I can, Mrs. Audeley. You like things to be done properly. And you are quite skilled at making the vision a reality."

"You flatter me," said Mrs. Audeley. "I'm surprised you entrusted any of this planning to a country mouse who hasn't had a proper London visit in years."

"Hmm...well, I daresay Richards did most of it," said Lord Kendall with a twinkle in his eye. "And furthermore, I see that your white soup may have one detractor." He nodded towards Lady Comfort, halfway down the long table, whose pinched face looked as if she had swallowed a thimbleful of vinegar.

"Poor Lady Comfort," said Mrs. Audeley in low tones. "No doubt she regrets refusing to organise this ball for you. It would have been a triumph for her."

"She would have said no to the peacock feathers."

"Then for Penelope's sake, I am glad I could help make the ball just as she would like it. Oh, I see that Mr. Tavinstock escorted her in for dinner. How pleasant of him."

"I took the liberty of informing certain gentlemen which dances they were to solicit from her. Tavinstock seemed like a suitable candidate to keep her entertained at dinner without letting her get into too much mischief."

Mrs. Audeley shook her head. "You, my lord, are a very managing man."

"Better that then have her cornered by an old *roué* like Solomon Digby."

"I suppose," said Mrs. Audeley, her pink lips pursing thoughtfully. "But she must fight her own battles at some point. Whatever her faults, Penelope is spirited enough to send a man like Solomon Digby about his business."

"You speak as if you admire that quality."

"I do admire it. If only I had been more forthright at her age, I would never—"

The earl leant a little closer. "What was that, Mrs. Audeley?"

Mrs. Audeley shook her head. That was a thought she had never meant to voice. She looked back down the long table and saw Lady Comfort continuing to glare at her. Clearly, the earl's attentions to her had not escaped notice. Indeed, the high-ranking duchess on Lord Kendall's left was being entirely neglected and had resorted to speaking loudly to the gentleman on her opposite side about the sad lack of good company in the metropolis.

"You must stop speaking to me," she admonished the earl, "and do your duty as a host."

Lord Kendall sighed. "Of course, you are right. As the old saying goes, 'duty before pleasure.'" He gave Mrs. Audeley a warm, lingering glance and then turned to the duchess and begged her to tell him what were the best watering spots in London.

Following the supper, Mrs. Audeley returned to the ballroom and discovered that her anonymity had disappeared with the dinner plates. She caught more than a dozen whispers of her name behind painted fans and beneath raised monocles as the seasoned denizens of London looked her over and talked behind her back. Holding her head high, Mrs. Audeley stood on the margin alone, trying to keep her eye fixed on Penelope's triumph as the belle of the ball and trying to keep her heart from fluttering too wildly.

Lord Kendall, recalled to his responsibilities as host, was kept in constant circulation, and without a large circle of acquaintances, Mrs. Audeley found herself at a loss where to set up camp. Although her name might be the word on everyone's lips, she herself was clearly not in demand as a conversational partner. It was hard to say for certain, but she thought that a few ladies turned their backs on her as she walked by, and one even seemed to be pulling her skirts out of the way of Mrs. Audeley's progress as if the widow were a stray dog or a leper.

Mrs. Haverstall was dancing with a lanky, middle-aged officer. She caught Mrs. Audeley's eye while doing the turns for the quadrille and, as soon as the dance was over, hurried off the dance floor to find her friend.

"How light you are on your feet!" declared Mrs. Audeley.

"Charming of you to say so, but come, dear friend, I must talk to you." Mrs. Haverstall took hold of Mrs. Audeley's gloved arm and led her off into a corner alcove, partially obscured by a potted plant.

"This must be grave news indeed," said Mrs. Audeley, "if we must hide away for you to tell it to me."

Mrs. Haverstall took a deep sigh. "I hate to be the bearer of it. But my dear friend, there is a rumour spreading around the ballroom that you are Lord Kendall's mistress."

Mrs. Audeley felt a tremor of cold seize her, making it difficult to move or talk. "Is that so?"

Mrs. Haverstall put an arm about her shoulder. "I'm afraid that Lady Comfort may be the instigator of the rumour, but dancing with the Duke of Warrenton did you no favours. He is rumoured to be a rake and enjoys making his way into the scandal sheets."

A wave of heat came crashing down on the cold, and anger overtook the numbness. "How exactly does she do it? Sidle up to someone and say, 'Have you heard that Lord Kendall has taken a country mouse for a mistress? Mrs. Audeley's the name.'"

"Oh no," said Mrs. Haverstall, "she is far more subtle than that. A word here about how surprised she is to see Lord Kendall neglecting his duties as host. A word there about how strange it is that Lord Kendall should own your townhouse on the edge of Grosvenor Square."

"Pardon?"

"Is it not true then? Lady Comfort has been telling people that Lord Kendall purchased the house you are staying in."

"I don't know." The room was whirling with the motion of the dancers and the heat from the hundreds of bodies packed into it. "He didn't say. Although it would certainly be strange to have my son in residence if I were a *kept* woman."

"Whether or not he did purchase the house, his attentions to you have been marked enough that Lady Comfort's insinuations have the ring of truth."

"Yes. I see that." It was so apparent to her now that she felt like a green girl for not having seen it before.

"The only other explanation could be that he's courting you in earnest. But Lord Kendall has had the pick of the ton for twenty-five years without any hints that he is looking for matrimony. He's avoided every trap that's been laid for him—including one by Lady Comfort's own sister. The general opinion is that he is a confirmed bachelor by now."

Mrs. Audeley swallowed. "Thank you for telling me, Clarissa." The leaves of the potted plant outside the alcove provided far too little coverage for the shame she felt. She wanted to sink into the ground and disappear rather than have to walk past the knowing smirks of all London.

Her friend looked at her anxiously. "Unpleasant as it is, I felt you ought to know. My dear, you look a little pale. Would you like Ned and I to take you home in our carriage?"

"I...yes, in a few minutes. But there is someone I must speak to before I leave."

As Mrs. Haverstall pressed her hand and slipped away to find Ned and order the carriage, Mrs. Audeley braced herself for the interview she was determined to have. She would not leave Kendall House until she had spoken a few candid words with his lordship, the Earl of Kendall.

CHAPTER TWENTY-SIX

Candour

M RS. AUDELEY HAD ENOUGH sense not to walk up to Lord Kendall in the crowded ballroom and draw him off into a private alcove for a *tête-à-tête*. No, that would only fan the flames of speculation and seal her status as his *chère amie*. Instead, she skirted the wall of the ballroom until she reached the door and discovered Mr. Richards hovering in the background, without any real tasks for the evening but determined to be of use should the occasion arise.

"Richards," she said, composing her face with a smile, "would you be so good as to tell his lordship that I need to speak with him in the study about an urgent matter?"

"Of course, Mrs. Audeley," said the slight man with white hair. No doubt he thought something had gone amiss with the punch, or the candles, or the musicians. He gave a half bow and headed for the ballroom while Mrs. Audeley let herself into the study which, by now, had become as familiar to her as her parlour in Upper Cross. She took a seat in one of the chairs beside the fireplace, not having the temerity to sit in the earl's own chair behind the desk, and warmed her slipper-clad toes while she waited.

It was a mere five minutes before Lord Kendall entered the study, a look of concern on his face. "Mrs. Audeley, what is it?"

She stood to face him. "I am sorry to bother you, my lord, but I am leaving the ball early, and I need to tell you why."

He raised an eyebrow, the firelight glinting off the flecks of silver in his dark hair.

"Lady Comfort has been spreading it about that I am your mistress, and the rumours have made it decidedly uncomfortable for me to continue in the ballroom.

The muscles in Lord Kendall's jaw twitched violently. "Arabella is a vicious witch. I'll speak with her. She'll take it back—and apologise to you and every person on whom she's vomited her venom."

"It's not just Lady Comfort—I'm afraid that we have spent too much time in each other's company, and it has been re-marked upon by others." Her voice wavered as she spoke. "The Duke of Warrenton mentioned it at the theatre, and I'm certain he's not the only one to have taken notice. I am horribly ashamed—"

Lord Kendall took two strides and put himself face to face with Mrs. Audeley. He gathered her gloved hands in his and pressed them gently. "No need for that. I'm the one who has been a selfish beast. You are so cordial and kind and comfortable I wanted to spend time with you. And so I did. Without any regard for your reputation and what society would say. Can you forgive me?"

Mrs. Audeley's legs trembled. His thumb was rubbing gently over the back of her gloved hand, stealing her ability to think clearly. She desperately wanted to accept the apology and see what else Lord Kendall had to say. But there was another matter that must be broached. "Are you the owner of the house I'm leasing?"

Lord Kendall froze. "Yes, I am."

"And did you pay my bills at the modiste?"

His eyes darted away from hers. "Only a few of them."

She pulled her hands away. "Don't you see? It's not just conversation between us now—it's money. In the eyes of Lady Comfort and the rest of them, it's incontrovertible proof. Why did you do it?"

A look of dismay came into Lord Kendall's blue eyes. "I meant nothing untoward by it. You had simply been so kind to assist with Penny. I knew the trip to London was a terrible expense, and I wanted to make things easier for you."

"But you're a man of the world. You know that a gentleman cannot open his pocketbook for an unmarried woman without tongues wagging."

"Well, devil take it, I'll make them stop their mouths." Without warning, Lord Kendall seized hold of Mrs. Audeley and pulled her tightly against him. His lips came down on hers in an ardent kiss. The desire in his lips was fierce and uncontained, but the kiss lasted no longer than a second before Mrs. Audeley pushed him away. Her blood raced with the heat of a thousand suns and her face flamed like noonday.

"Please, my lord!"

"I mean to marry you," he said, breathing heavily, his hands still about her waist.

"Oh, you do, do you? And now that you've paid my way in London, I have no choice in the matter?"

His hands fell to his sides and a low growl came from his throat. "That is not what I meant."

Mrs. Audeley stepped away, putting space between them. She folded her arms across her bosom protectively and turned her back to face the fire. It was a few minutes before she trusted herself to speak, and even when she did, she could not look into his eyes and continued to stare into the hearth. "When I was eighteen years old, I had a dream of coming to London. My parents were poor as church mice. My father was a solicitor, but Mr. Audeley was his only well-paying client. My parents told me that the dresses and the carriage and the lodging were above our touch. But then somehow over the course of Christmas, they changed their minds. They sent me to London, and I had my season."

Mrs. Audeley straightened her shoulders. "I would never have attracted notice from an earl like you, but I had my share of admirers. I had no dowry, however, and nothing came of any of them. When I returned to Upper Cross, Mr. Audeley was there waiting. My father told me the truth then—that Mr. Audeley had paid for my season. He knew I was keen to go to London, and so he had arranged with my parents that I should have my fun and my finery and that we would be wed when I returned."

Lord Kendall growled. "And you said yes?"

"What else could I say? I had already spent his money. I had no choice." She whirled around again to face him. "And now here I am again—with all my choices taken away."

"I never meant—"

"I won't make the same mistake this time." Her tone was cordial but firm. "I thank you for your consideration in securing my lodging. I thank you for your generosity in expanding my wardrobe. Tomorrow, I shall be returning to Derbyshire."

Lord Kendall raked his hand through his silver-flecked hair. "Mrs. Audeley, please consider what will be said. You must allow me to put the rumours to rest and make this right."

"It is too late for that, my lord."

And with that, Mrs. Audeley went to retrieve her wrap and head home in the Haverstall carriage, turning back only long enough to beg Lord Kendall to inform Gyles that she was feeling indisposed and had made her own way home.

CHAPTER TWENTY-SEVEN

Intruder

T HE BUSINESS OF SMILING and nodding when one's heart has been shredded to mincemeat is an excruciating one. Lord Kendall only managed to carry it off by reminding himself that he was the guardian of three orphan girls whom he had a duty to launch creditably into society. It would do Penny no favours if he were to abandon his role as host and lock himself in his study while the ball-goers wore out their slippers without him.

It was the outside of enough, however, that he was forced to deal with Lady Comfort's continued presence. He dropped a word in Sir Oliver's ear that his wife had had too much punch and was making a cake of herself in front of Lady Sefton, and the befuddled fellow rounded up Cassie and Arabella and—despite their voluble protests—bundled them into a carriage to take them home.

Flushed and exhilarated, Penny finished every set on her full dance card, her feet as light as a fairy sprite. Gyles led her out for the final set of country dances, and as the ball came to an end, she was, for once, in perfect charity with her odious uncle.

As the last bars of music sounded, the whorls of flowers and flourishes that had been drawn on the ballroom floor had disappeared into streaks of dirty chalk. The peacock feathers and white roses drooped in the large urns, looking as weary as Lord Kendall's battered heart.

He pasted on a jovial smile as he bid farewell to the last of the guests, the cold November air shutting the front door on the last leave-taking. When he turned around, he saw that Penny, Gyles, and a horde of liveried footmen were all that was left. Penny was dancing around the floor dreamily reliving her triumph, Gyles was inspecting the hardihood of the roses in the vases, and the footmen were removing empty platters, clearing half-full punch glasses, and sweeping up crumbs and bits of torn lace.

"Uncle Bertie! Uncle Bertie!"

Lord Kendall wandered down the hallway and looked up the staircase in surprise. There were Ginny and Milly, hand in hand, squealing as they stood on their tiptoes and looked over the bannister.

"Girls," groaned Lord Kendall. "It's late. Why have you not gone to bed?"

"Uncle Bertie," said Ginny anxiously. "We have something unpleasant to tell you."

Lord Kendall could think of nothing more unpleasant than what he had suffered less than an hour ago in his study.

"Can't it wait till morning?"

"No, Uncle Bertie!" said Milly. "It most certainly cannot."

By now, Penelope and Gyles had joined the earl at the foot of the stairs.

"Out with it then."

Ginny folded her hands in front of her as if she were about to give a recitation for a schoolteacher. "A fat man in a mauve waistcoat came upstairs into the family quarters where Miss Lymington was reading to us in the schoolroom."

"A man?" gasped Penelope.

"He was foxed," said little Milly sagely.

Lord Kendall's face filled with alarm, and he began to take the stairs two at a time. "Are you all right? Did he harm you?"

"No," said Ginny staunchly, "he hardly noticed us. It was Miss Lymington who caught his attention."

"He called her a great many names," said Milly, "and chased her round and round the schoolroom table."

"Miss Lymington?" echoed Gyles. He had begun to rush up the stairs as well. "Is she hurt?"

"No," said Ginny. "Milly and I took a curtain ribbon and tied it to the bottom of the table and held onto the other end, and when he came raging round that direction, he tripped and fell flat on his face."

"I think he was already unconscious," said Milly, "but I broke my slate over his head while he was lying there and gave him a couple hard kicks just to be sure."

"But where is he now?" asked Lord Kendall, scooping Milly up in one arm and throwing his other arm about Ginny's shoulders.

"Why, in the schoolroom, of course!" said Ginny. "We found more curtain ribbons and tied him to a chair, and Miss Lymington is standing guard over him while we came to find you."

At this, they all made a pell-mell rush for the next flight of stairs that led up to the schoolroom. Lord Kendall deposited Milly on the carpet in the hallway and pushed open the door only to discover the heart-shaped face of Miss Lymington glaring most unlovingly at a trussed-up Solomon Digby while she held a ruler menacingly and ordered him not to move a muscle.

"Miss Lymington," cried Gyles, pushing past him to reach the side of the governess-cum-Amazon. "Are you unhurt?"

"Quite unhurt," she said, her eyes flashing sparks, "but Mr. Digby here might not be able to say the same."

"He might not be able to say anything at all, considering that you've gagged him with five layers of ribbons," observed Lord Kendall.

"I did not want him to shout and draw attention to the other guests."

"Very resourceful of you, Miss Lymington," said Gyles with feeling.

"Surely his shouting will not matter now," said Penelope. "We must find out why he came upstairs."

Lord Kendall was already engaged in unwinding the ribbon that bound Mr. Digby's jaws. His touch was none too gentle, and Mr. Digby groaned every time the earl's hands knocked against the large goose egg forming on his forehead. "Mr. Digby," said Lord Kendall sternly, once the man's ability to speak had been restored, "I invited you into my house as a guest. Explain to me why you came upstairs and assaulted my nieces and their governess."

"Governess!" said Mr. Digby, as if he had been insulted. "That's rich, Kendall. This girl here is none other than Louisa Lymington, the ward of the Duke of Warrenton."

The three girls and Gyles gasped simultaneously while the beauty with the honey-gold hair set her lips in a firm line.

"I am aware," said the earl coldly. "And what, pray tell, is that to you?"

CHAPTER TWENTY-EIGHT

Lady Louisa

"WHAT IS IT TO *me*?" echoed Mr. Digby. "The chit's been missing for months. Warrenton keeps putting me off—says she's in the country, gone to Scotland, suffering the toothache. When all the time, here she is living under your roof. Imagine my shock when I saw her peering over the bannister out of the shadows upstairs as I entered your house tonight. Why, I ought to call you out, you cur!"

"I'm unclear why you would have that responsibility or privilege."

"Because the gel's promised to me! As good as engaged. We could be married tomorrow."

"I beg to differ," said Lady Louisa, raising her ruler like a truncheon. Lord Kendall had no doubts that she would use it if further provoked. "I have never agreed to marry you, and I shall waste away my life in the wilds of Yorkshire before I do so."

"Oh, come now," wheedled Mr. Digby. "You were sweet as cream to me the last time I saw you."

"That," said Lady Louisa tartly, "was to lull you into a false sense of security so that I could escape my uncle's house."

"But I don't understand!" said Penelope. "Why would your uncle force you to marry this shocking excuse for a man?"

"Because my uncle is a greedy beast," said Lady Louisa in a tone of cool disdain. "He inherited the dukedom a couple years ago when my father died, but the estate is bankrupt. My inheritance comes through my mother's side, and although I can't touch it until I come into my majority, neither can he. The only person who can is a husband. So, my uncle made a secret arrangement with Mr. Digby that if he allowed him to marry me, they would split my money once the marriage vows were said."

"How do you know that?" demanded Mr. Digby.

Lady Louisa rolled her eyes at the rotund man still tied to the chair. "I have my wits about me, and I know how to listen at keyholes."

"But how did you become a governess?" asked Gyles, genuinely shocked by the latest turn of events and unsure how to relate to the newly discovered daughter of a duke.

"I answered an advertisement in the newspaper and slipped out of my uncle's house with one trunk, my pin money, and a good head on my shoulders. Then, I took the post to Yorkshire—"

"And as there were no other promising candidates to educate my nieces, I hired you," said Lord Kendall. It had certainly complicated matters. He did not like to remember the scene when he realised his new governess' identity and confronted her with it.

"It would have suited my purposes to stay in Yorkshire until I came of age," said Lady Louisa, turning on the earl, "but you *would* insist that I return to town. All I needed was six more months until I am free from my uncle's control."

"It is not unreasonable to expect a governess to stay in the vicinity of her charges."

"Yes, but Mr. Digby would never have discovered me if I had remained in Yorkshire." She waved the ruler fiercely at the prisoner. "And now he will go to my uncle Warrenton as soon as we release him. My uncle will find me, and I shall be wholly in his power once again."

"Surely there is something we can do," said Gyles.

Penelope clapped her hands together. "I have it! Uncle Bertie must marry Miss Lymington!"

Lord Kendall took a step backwards. Lady Louisa's perfectly bowed lips curved in a moue of derision.

"But don't you see," continued Penelope, "it's just the thing! If Uncle Bertie married Miss Lymington, then Mr. Digby would be quite out of luck. And the Duke of Warrenton couldn't do a thing about it. Uncle Bertie has coffers of money, and I'm sure he wouldn't touch Miss Lymington's fortune. How could anyone have any objection to that plan?"

"The principals might," said Gyles, looking anxiously from Lady Louisa to Lord Kendall.

"*I* object!" bellowed Mr. Digby, causing Penny to stuff the ribbon gag back into his mouth and wind it thrice about his head. He glared fiercely at her, muttering indistinct threats and garbled insults.

"I suppose Lord Kendall is marginally preferable," said Lady Louisa. "At least *he* doesn't wear shockingly hideous waistcoats, even though he is also old enough to be my father." She grimaced.

"No." declared Lord Kendall, crossing his arms across his chest, his shoulders straining at the seams of his ballroom jacket. "Absolutely not."

"But think of poor Miss Lymington," pleaded Ginny. "How can you leave her to her fate?"

"She's quite pretty," observed Milly. "The innkeeper wouldn't have pinched her bottom if she weren't."

"I have no intention of marrying—"

"But why not?"

"It's a capital idea."

"I've always wanted an aunt."

"—anyone other than Mrs. Audeley!"

The noise in the room dropped to a dead silence.

Lord Kendall glanced apologetically at Gyles Audeley. After all, it could hardly be comfortable to hear someone announce his intentions towards one's mother in such a public setting.

"So that's the way the wind blows," said Gyles, locking eyes with him, but not unduly disturbed.

"I adore Mrs. Audeley!" said Penelope. "If you're to marry her, then Miss Lymington had better find another gentleman to rescue her."

"I've done quite well rescuing myself so far," said Miss Lymington without a hint of sweetness.

"Yes, well, Mrs. Audeley may not be keen on the idea," said Lord Kendall hastily. "In fact, I rather think she opposes it."

Mr. Digby, who had managed to squirm his way out of the poorly tied gag, took this moment to shove his own oar in. "Can't see why. Would make an honest woman of her. Not sure why she'd prefer to remain your mistress—"

Before Mr. Digby could finish his statement, Lord Kendall rendered him incapable of speaking, this time with a firm blow to the jaw rather than a few yards of wide ribbon.

"Oh!" squealed all his nieces.

"I think it's time you all went to bed," said Lord Kendall firmly, quelling the girls' antics with an unusual sternness in his bright blue eyes. "Lady Louisa, we'll speak in the morning. Gyles, could you send two footmen up on your way out? When Mr. Digby wakes up, I don't want him anywhere near this house."

Chapter Twenty-Nine

Disappearance

M RS. AUDELEY SPENT A fitful night. She had poured out her further discoveries to Clarissa Haverstall in the carriage while Ned Haverstall looked out the window and stoically pretended not to listen.

"But, dearest," Mrs. Haverstall had said. "Are you certain that the situations are so similar? Lord Kendall is surely far more solicitous of your comfort and wishes than Mr. Audeley was."

"He is now, but who can say whether that would change. The way he has managed things bodes ill for him consulting my preferences later. And his proposal—I could not think of a less favourable wording. 'I mean to marry you.' Without any expression of sentiment on his part or care for my own feelings."

"In his defence," Ned Haverstall had interrupted, feeling called upon to defend his own sex, "he may not have had time to plan out the proper phrasing."

But Mrs. Audeley had dismissed that objection out of hand. And when she arrived back at the townhouse, she glanced dismally around at the furnishings and carved mouldings that belonged to Lord Kendall and escaped up the stairs to her room. At least she would be gone tomorrow, without her surroundings a constant reminder of her imprudence.

Sleep was a long time coming. Mrs. Audeley's mind swung like a pendulum between her outraged sensibilities and her inexplicable longing for matters to turn out...differently.

It had been unconscionable and highhanded of Lord Kendall to arrange her lodging and wardrobe without a word to her. But at the same time, that kiss in the study was unlike anything she had ever experienced. The ardent longing on Lord Kendall's lips had heated her like a warm breath on long-banked embers. Hours had passed since the moment, and still the glow refused to die down. Her late husband had never kissed her like...that.

In the morning, however, Mrs. Audeley's indignation returned. She looked for Gyles at the breakfast table to inform him of their imminent departure, but it seemed that, after a late night, he was still abed. At ten o'clock, he had still not appeared. She rang for Garrick and told him to ask Gyles to wait on her in the drawing room. Garrick shuffled his feet uncomfortably, a peculiar stance for a normally unflappable butler.

"What is it?"

"Mr. Audeley never returned home last night."

Mrs. Audeley's face paled. She reached for the edge of the console table to steady herself. "Never returned?" She supposed it was possible that a young man might be seduced into games of dice and haunts of ill repute, drinking his way into an unseemly slumber. But Gyles had never shown evidence of being that type.

"And the carriage?"

"No sign of it either."

"Good heavens!" The only explanations were that Gyles had been set upon by footpads on his short journey home or that he had spent the night at Kendall House. "Garrick, I'm going out." Seizing a shawl, Mrs. Audeley stepped out onto the pavement and began a brisk and worried walk to the inner circle of Grosvenor Square.

She sounded the knocker. Lord Kendall's butler recognized her immediately and ushered her into the drawing room without standing on ceremony. It was only when she was standing in front of the master of the house that she realised she had come all this way without a bonnet, without a lace cap, or indeed, without any head covering at all.

"Good morning, Mrs. Audeley," said Lord Kendall. She noticed that his chiselled features were taut and his pleasantries laboured. "To what do I owe the honour of your company?"

She cast down her eyes. "I suppose it is rather a shock to see me, since I told you I would be returning to Derbyshire today, but the truth of the matter is I can't find Gyles anywhere."

"Gyles?" His eyebrows lifted. "Well, he's certainly not here. I haven't laid eyes on him since last night. We've our own missing person this morning, however. You haven't, perchance, caught sight of Miss Lymington, have you?"

Mrs. Audeley shook her head. "How peculiar that they should both be missing!" She folded her hands and discovered that she'd left the house without gloves as well. "You wouldn't mind if I paid a visit to Gyles' rosebush, would you? To see if he's tending it?"

"Of course not. Make yourself at home."

Mrs. Audeley had no sooner stepped outside the drawing room than she was beset by a chorus of girlish cries echoing across the marble floors of the entrance hall.

"Mrs. Audeley, have you heard the horrible news?"

"Lady Louisa has been spirited away!"

"Ginny thinks it's Mr. Digby that did it, but *I* think it's the wicked uncle!"

"Girls, girls," said Mrs. Audeley, putting her arms about the shoulders of the two younger ones. "Who is Lady Louisa? And what has happened?"

As Mrs. Audeley listened attentively, Penelope spun the dire tale of the governess who was really a duke's daughter, of her nefarious uncle's plot, and of the vulgar intruder abovestairs yesterevening.

"And Uncle Bertie refused to marry her to save her from her predicament," announced Ginny.

"Which is no surprise," said Milly, "as he only wants to marry—"

Lord Kendall cleared his throat. "We can do without my exact words, Milly."

"Goodness!" said Mrs. Audeley, and her hand flew to her mouth to stifle a gasp. "Do you think that's where Gyles is? That he's offered to marry Lady Louisa to save her from her wicked uncle?"

"Is that how I'm being styled?" asked a roguish voice, and the party of ladies and Lord Kendall looked up to see that the Duke of Warrenton had manoeuvred past the butler and shouldered his way into the entrance hall of Kendall House.

CHAPTER THIRTY

An Accord

"WHAT ARE *YOU* DOING here?" demanded Mrs. Audeley.

"I've had a visit from Solomon Digby this morning," the Duke of Warrenton announced coolly. "Rather early in the morning, too, for Digby. He's usually not awake till teatime."

"He must have had something important to convey." Lord Kendall stepped in front of the ladies to keep the conversation between himself and the Duke of Warrenton.

"*He* certainly thought it was. Said that the Earl of Kendall has been harbouring my runaway ward."

"Harbouring is not the term I would use."

"He claims she's your governess."

"I did hire her as such."

"How comical! I knew Louisa was a superb actress, but to think that she should have taken you in. I wonder that you did not see through her lack of skills immediately."

"Miss Lymington is an excellent governess," objected Ginny, stepping around her uncle to defend the absent Lady Louisa. "She knows French and Italian and paints beautifully."

"In fact," said Milly, opening her blue eyes as wide as possible, "I think she is a far better governess than you are an uncle."

"That would not be difficult," said Warrenton dryly. "But as I *am* her uncle and her guardian in court of law, she is obliged to obey me. Where is she, Kendall?"

Lord Kendall raked a hand through his silvery black hair. "That's the question, Warrenton. Nobody knows."

"Mrs. Audeley is afraid she's run off with Gyles," said Penelope helpfully, "but that's quite impossible. Gyles is irrevocably devoted to me."

"How distressing," said the duke. "Although I tend to find that masculine devotion is often of a more temporary nature."

"Seeing as we know nothing of her whereabouts," said Lord Kendall, striving manfully to regain control of the situation, "you might as well take yourself off, Warrenton."

As this drama unfolded near the Kendall House door, Mr. Richards, the earl's secretary, entered from the hallway and handed a folded piece of paper to Mrs. Audeley. It was crisp and white but with a puzzling pattern of dirt around the edges. "Mr. Audeley asked for paper and pen last night," Richards said in low undertones, "and I discovered this note in the soil next to his rose bush this morning."

Mrs. Audeley seized the paper and unfolded it. Her eyes scanned it rapidly, her heart beating a rapid tattoo in her breast. "I am sorry, Penelope," she said, "but I am afraid my earlier suspicions are confirmed. Gyles has disappeared with Lady Louisa, and this note implies that they intend to be married."

Lord Kendall reached for the note so he could confirm the contents with his own eyes, but Mrs. Audeley waved him away and folded the note tightly into her palm.

Penelope let out a loud wail and started to crumple to the floor, having the presence of mind to angle herself towards her guardian so that he could more easily catch her during her nervous collapse. Irritably, Lord Kendall hoisted the clearly conscious Penelope into his arms and carried her into the drawing room to lay her on the sofa, while Milly, Ginny, and white-haired Richards followed, clucking with dismay like a brood of hens.

"So, that minx has made off with your son," said the duke, approaching Mrs. Audeley in the entrance hall. He took her bare hand in his and pressed it. "What do you mean to do about it?"

"Do? I'm not sure there's anything we can do. We don't even know where they've gone."

"Scotland," said Warrenton succinctly. "I'd stake money on it, if I had any."

"Perhaps you could stake Lady Louisa's money on it," said Mrs. Audeley tartly. She was horrified by the idea of a match between kind-hearted Gyles and the haughty Lady Louisa, but it did no good to admit as much to Warrenton.

"Yes, well, I mean to. She's six months away from coming of age, and I shan't let her slip through my fingers so easily."

He trailed his own fingers along her forearm as he spoke. "No gloves, Mrs. Audeley? And no cap?" He leaned in closer so that his lips almost grazed her ear. "If I didn't know better, I would think you were very *at home* with Lord Kendall."

Mrs. Audeley pulled away, just in time to see Lord Kendall entering the room with raised eyebrows. A feeling of guilt came over her even though she knew she had done nothing wrong. What was Lord Kendall thinking of her? "His grace thinks they are bound for Scotland," she stated hurriedly,

"I'll intercept them, of course," said Warrenton smoothly.

"And then what?" Mrs. Audeley demanded.

"Bring Louisa back with me. As a fallen woman, she'll have no choice but to marry Digby to salvage her reputation."

"Gyles would never let you do such a thing."

A humorous smile played over the duke's lips. "I think I'm well equipped to handle a young pup like that."

A hundred scenarios played through Mrs. Audeley's mind, most of them involving Gyles playing the hero with fists, sword, or pistol and dying a hero's death at the hands of the far more experienced duke. "I'm going with you," she declared fiercely.

"How charming!" said Warrenton giving her a wolfish smile. "I own, I would be glad of the company. A trip to Scotland can be a lonely business."

"A word, Mrs. Audeley," said Lord Kendall, his voice short and clipped. While Warrenton looked on with a provoking smile, the earl drew the lady over into a corner. "You cannot travel alone with Warrenton," he whispered fiercely. "Think of your reputation."

"My reputation is already ruined, my lord, thanks to our friendship."

"It will be ruined in reality as well as rumour if Warrenton has his way with you."

"Are you forbidding me to go?" There was a light of challenge in Mrs. Audeley's eyes, daring him to take this decision away from her.

"No," said Lord Kendall hoarsely, his blue eyes glinting like burnished steel. "But if you *are* going, then I'm coming with you."

CHAPTER THIRTY-ONE

The Chase

MRS. AUDELEY MADE NO argument to Lord Kendall joining the expedition, and once the plan was settled, the earl sprang into action. He sent out runners and discovered that a carriage matching the description of the Audeley conveyance had been seen leaving London during the early hours of the morning. As expected, its direction was northward. Meanwhile, the Duke of Warrenton sent round a note to his house for his valet to pack him a trunk. Then, he took up a seat in the Kendall drawing room, leaning nonchalantly against the back of the settee as he read the borrowed newspaper.

Lord Kendall sent Mrs. Audeley back to her house in his carriage where she packed a small trunk and attired herself properly in gloves, cap, bonnet, and travelling dress. She had no lady's maid in service as she was used to attending to her own attire, but when she returned to Kendall House, she discovered that the earl had made arrangements for Penelope's maid to accompany them.

"But how shall I dress my hair while you are gone?" wailed Penny, upset to have her abigail drafted into service without warning.

"Have one of your sisters do it for you," replied Lord Kendall callously.

"A word, Lord Kendall," said Mrs. Audeley. Once again, they moved into the corner, but this time it was Mrs. Audeley doing the whispering. "Stop behaving like an ogre to Penelope. I have no need of her maid."

Lord Kendall crossed his arms. "I say that you do. You will not travel alone in a carriage with two gentlemen."

Mrs. Audeley jutted her chin out firmly. "If you are so concerned for propriety, how can you leave the girls here by themselves without a governess or guardian?"

"They have Mrs. Gale to look after them."

"Oh, fustian!" Mrs. Audeley was becoming increasingly infuriated with the managing man who stood in front of her. "She wouldn't hear them leave the house if they slammed the door on their way out. They'll be romping around the metropolis by the time you get back, getting up to all sorts of sad capers."

"Then what would you suggest I do?" demanded Lord Kendall from between gritted teeth. "I have a dearth of female relatives to serve as chaperones in my absence."

Mrs. Audeley would not back down from his steely-eyed stare. "Invite Clarissa Haverstall."

"Why would she exert herself?"

"As a particular favour to *me*. I'll ask her to come round."

Lord Kendall gave grudging assent to this, and as Mrs. Audeley anticipated, her old friend did not fail her. Within a quarter of an hour after the note's receipt, she had arrived in her carriage and kindly offered to stay with the girls until their guardian's return. "Ned will be here too," she said soothingly, "and all will be well taken care of. I can only pray you find Gyles in time to save him from a serious misstep."

Mrs. Audeley swallowed. It was entirely possible that the misstep was already unavoidable. Gyles had set out alone with a noblewoman in a closed carriage, and if they did not catch up with them before nightfall, he would be obliged to offer for her. Indeed, given the choice of Gyles and Solomon Digby, Lady Louisa could hardly fail to choose Gyles. Mrs. Audeley had been looking forward to gaining a daughter-in-law in London, but she gravely doubted that Lady Louisa's imperious ways would sort well with Gyles' gentle and romantic nature. If only he had not resolved to play knight-errant!

The Duke of Warrenton clearly had no urgent desire to over-take the couple in a timely fashion. It was as if he *wanted* his niece to be ruined. If he had been a more concerned uncle, he would have been riding hell for leather, but as it was, he ordered a cup of chocolate from the staff at Kendall House and allowed Lord Kendall and Mrs. Audeley to wrangle their way into readiness. It was nearly noon before they climbed into the carriage to set out on the rescue mission.

Inside the carriage, Penelope's dark-browed maid, Jeanette, shared the forward-facing seat with Mrs. Audeley while both gentlemen sat opposite in cramped proximity. Conversation was strained or absent entirely. The Duke of Warrenton made a few sallies, but Mrs. Audeley was in no mood for banter, and Lord Kendall was curt and distant. Mrs. Audeley, the party most concerned with speed, gave Lord Kendall's coachman or-ders to drive swiftly up the Great North Road.

When they arrived at a coaching inn to change horses, Lord Kendall leaped out of the carriage to speak with the ostler. Mrs.

Audeley and Jeanette went to use the necessary and returned to find the duke lounging on the bench and stretching his limbs like a large feline.

"Have you inquired about passing carriages?" asked Mrs. Audeley.

"Kendall's quite capable of handling that," said the duke with a yawn. "And I don't have the coin to waste on rewarding sharp-eyed stableboys."

"So, you're happy to have someone else manage everything for you?"

"Why shouldn't I be? Kendall enjoys sorting things and I enjoy having them sorted."

Mrs. Audeley blinked at this and adjusted the ribbons of her white-trimmed bonnet. Indeed, it was quite pleasant not to have to deal with the ostler or innkeeper themselves while Lord Kendall bore the brunt of the cold November wind and the fact-finding questions, but all the same, she felt as if she should be *doing* something.

The carriage flung open, and Lord Kendall climbed back inside.

"How are the new cattle?" asked Warrenton.

"Passable," said Lord Kendall, rubbing his cold hands together. "Although I found a better pair in the stable—your blacks, Mrs. Audeley."

Mrs. Audeley clapped her hands. "So! They *did* change horses here."

"Yes, the stable boy remembers your coachman. A big florid fellow by the name of John?"

Mrs. Audeley nodded.

"The carriage came through before sunrise. It looks as if we're eight hours behind them."

"Dear me," said the Duke of Warrenton with a sardonic smile at Mrs. Audeley. "Unless their carriage overturns, there's no possibility of catching them before nightfall. At least they have four or five days' travel before they reach Scotland. If Kendall keeps everything running like clockwork, we'll surely overtake them before they can find an anvil parson."

"It would serve you right if Gyles did marry your niece," said Mrs. Audeley in crisp tones, "and you lose all hope of getting your hands on her inheritance."

"Ah, but then *you* would be forced to have her for a daughter-in-law," replied the duke, "and although you might appear meek, Mrs. Audeley, I think you would not take kindly to a minx like Louisa leading your son about by the nose."

CHAPTER THIRTY-TWO

The Dilemma

TRUE TO PREDICTION, LORD Kendall's carriage did not catch up with their quarry that day. Lord Kendall pushed each pair of horses to their limit before hiring new ones at the posting stops. They carried on into the evening, the carriage lanterns casting an eerie glow on their faces inside the coach. The Duke of Warrenton crossed his arms and fell asleep. The maid Jeanette laid her head back against the squabs and followed suit. But Lord Kendall and Mrs. Audeley kept silent vigil in the coach.

The air grew thick with the silence between them. Mrs. Audeley wondered a few times if Lord Kendall might return to their conversation in the study the previous evening, but the constraint of Warrenton's snoring presence was enough to keep that topic at bay.

When it was nearly midnight, they arrived in Alconbury. Lord Kendall secured rooms at the inn and helped Mrs. Audeley, stiff and bone-weary, out of the carriage. Mrs. Audeley blinked in the bright lights of the innyard and stifled a yawn with her hand. She was too tired to inquire into the specifics of their lodging and followed like a child as Lord Kendall escorted her to the back of the inn.

"Did you happen to secure a room for me as well?" asked Warrenton, fully alive in the darkest hour of the evening as creatures of the night are wont to be.

"You're sharing with me," said Lord Kendall curtly.

"Ah," said the duke. "I wonder, is that because the innkeeper ran short of rooms or because you'd like to know my whereabouts all through the night?"

Lord Kendall ignored that question. As Warrenton sauntered off to find some liquid refreshment, the earl deposited Mrs. Audeley at the foot of the staircase that led to her room. "Sleep well."

"I'm afraid I'll be too anxious to do much more than fret on my pillow. If we don't catch up to them before they reach Scotland, they'll tie the knot and Gyles will be leg-shackled for life to that..."

"Horribly despotic damsel."

"Exactly. But if we do catch them before they reach the border, then the duke will create a scandal broth so warm that it will scald us all. And although I cannot *like* Lady Louisa, I would hardly wish Solomon Digby upon her—"

Lord Kendall placed a finger against Mrs. Audeley's lips. "Sh. Stop dwelling upon it."

Mrs. Audeley swallowed and held perfectly still, her pink lips pressed against his rough index finger.

Lord Kendall smiled faintly and then let his hand slip away slowly. "Good night, Mrs. Audeley."

"Good night," she whispered.

Sleep came sooner than she expected. She shared a bed with Jeanette and woke early in the still-grey dawn. Her carriage dress was a little rumpled from the previous day, but Jeanette smoothed and shook it out as much as possible and then set to work on her hair. "It's not as if I shall be having callers today," objected Mrs. Audeley as the maid began coaxing the curls around her face.

"I daresay his grace and his lordship would appreciate the effort," said the French maid with a knowing smile. Mrs. Audeley refused to dignify that comment with any response, but she did look in the glass after Jeanette was finished and decided that, despite how she felt inside, she looked very well outside.

The second day of travel was more tedious than the first. Lord Kendall had inquired circumspectly at the inns in Alconbury about a young man and a young woman of Gyles and Louisa's descriptions, but no one remembered seeing them. One inn about a mile down the road remembered a change of horses being arranged by someone of the coachman John's description, and so they were able to conclude that their quarry had not lodged in Alconbury but had done so farther up the road.

The Duke of Warrenton had apparently drunk more than was good for him at the inn the previous night, for he had a sore head all morning and kept his more flirtatious comments to himself. They crossed the river at Wansford and ate a late nuncheon in Stamford. By the time they reached Grantham, it was nearing sunset. Mrs. Audeley thought it too soon to stop for the night, but Warrenton urged a rest. "Kendall's so dashed efficient with arranging new horses, that we've barely had time to get out of the carriage all day. I hardly think your son would know how to order around ostlers and get the best horses out of them. I daresay we'll catch them in the morning if we stay the night here."

Lord Kendall inquired at the largest inn and discovered that Mrs. Audeley's coachman had indeed traded a tired pair for a pair of fresh bays just about midday. "Headed north, I presume?"

The ostler scratched his head. "I don't rightly know, but it seemed that he were headed west toward Nottingham."

Warrenton thought the fellow's speculations nonsense. "Why would they leave the Great North Road? Does your son know anyone in Nottingham?"

"No," said Mrs. Audeley, lifting a gloved hand to her temple as she tried to think. "But Nottingham is on the way to Derbyshire. Do you think he might—"

"—be heading for Upper Cross?" interjected Lord Kendall. "Highly probable, I should say."

"Is that where you hail from?" Warrenton received a nod in the affirmative. "Well, I can't blame your son. Perhaps he's had enough of Louisa's sharp tongue, has decided to cry off, and needs somewhere to stow her. Should we turn west?"

"If we're wrong though," said Mrs. Audeley, "they'll reach the border before us and find an anvil parson, and it will be too late."

"What would you like to do, Mrs. Audeley?" asked Lord Kendall. He looked at her searchingly.

"Oh dear," said Mrs. Audeley, wringing her hands. "I suppose I must make the decision, mustn't I?"

"I wouldn't want to be accused of making it for you." His voice was unfailingly patient, but his words couldn't help but be pointed.

Mrs. Audeley took a deep breath. "Then let's turn west to Derbyshire."

It was another fifty miles to Upper Cross from Grantham, so they agreed to press on as far as Nottingham, lodge there, and then finish the journey the next day. That night, Mrs. Audeley could barely sleep, the weight of her decision weighing heavily upon her chest. If Lord Kendall had chosen the road, it would have been easy enough to blame him if matters turned out wrongly. But he had given her the choice, and she must abide by the consequences. What if she had chosen wrongly and lost her chance to intercept Gyles? She could not imagine the thought of her mild-mannered and quixotic son being riveted to a virago like Lady Louisa.

The following morning, they rose early and pursued the road to Upper Cross. As they drew nearer, Mrs. Audeley felt her stomach tie into knots. There were the bushes where Penny had thrown her half boots. There was the long drive leading down to the house. There was the front door and the entrance to the rose garden.

Lord Kendall's coachman pulled around to the open stables, and Mrs. Audeley let out a little gasp. There was her carriage, parked under the stable roof with the traces loose on the ground and the rented horses resting in the stalls.

"So, you guessed rightly, Mrs. Audeley!" said Warrenton triumphantly. He rose from his seat almost before the carriage came to a halt and was down the carriage steps. "If you'll pardon me, I'd like to be the first to greet my niece."

Lord Kendall assisted Mrs. Audeley in disembarking and instructed Penelope's maid to remain in the carriage until they sent for her. They walked towards the house, but before they reached the path leading to the front door, Lord Kendall seized

Mrs. Audeley's hand and drew her around the corner of the house into the perimeter of the rose garden. "A word, Mrs. Audeley, if I may."

CHAPTER THIRTY-THREE

An Offer

LORD KENDALL LEANED IN urgently to Mrs. Audeley. "Do you want me to offer for her?" It was a sacrifice of monumental proportions, but he was willing to make it if it would bring some glimmer of light back into her anxiety-stricken eyes.

She stared at him in shocked surprise. "Pardon? Offer for whom?"

"Lady Louisa. If we find her here with Gyles."

"But—why would you?" Mrs. Audeley spluttered. "She would never accept!"

"Oh, I daresay she could be convinced. When I first recognised her in Yorkshire, she told me in no uncertain terms that if I revealed her whereabouts to her uncle, she would shout it to the world that I had compromised her and force me to marry her. That's one of the reasons I departed for London so precipitously with Penelope. I didn't want to risk being in the same house as her in case she made good on her threat. And after this latest escapade, she has to marry *someone*. I may not be the paragon of perfection, but I'm a vast improvement on Solomon Digby." He looked at her gravely. "It would be one way of getting Gyles out of this scrape he's got himself into."

"B-but...marriage is so permanent."

"Indeed." That thought was beating a doleful drum in the back of Lord Kendall's mind.

"And Warrenton would never allow it."

"I can manage Warrenton."

"You mean you can buy him off."

Lord Kendall shrugged in acknowledgement. Having money was a convenient way of handling venial men like the Duke of Warrenton. If he offered Warrenton half the sum of Lady Louisa's inheritance, there would be no need for Solomon Digby.

"But think of the girls! Penelope will be horrified if you make Miss Lymington her aunt."

He chuckled dryly. "Penelope is always horrified by me. It will be no different than usual."

Mrs. Audeley began to gnaw her lower lip. "I daresay this is why you came along in the carriage. Lady Louisa is a beautiful young woman, and it's no wonder that you want—"

"Thunder and turf!" Lord Kendall dropped her gloved hand like a heated brick and ran his own hand through his silver-flecked hair. "Why must you misunderstand me so wilfully? My only reason for proposing such is to save your wretched boy. I don't *want* to marry Lady Louisa."

"You don't?"

"No," he said curtly.

"My, my! Where are you two hiding yourselves?" said a familiar and odious voice.

Lord Kendall's teeth ground together involuntarily, and he tried to silence the blood pulsing through his temples. He offered Mrs. Audeley his arm and propelled her out of the garden towards the front door. "Did you find them?"

"Yes and no," said Warrenton, standing on the stairs outside the front door. "I found Coachman John in the kitchen."

"And Gyles and Louisa?" asked Mrs. Audeley, anxiously.

Warrenton snorted. "Wait until you hear what the coachman has to say."

Alarmed, Mrs. Audeley let go of Lord Kendall, gathered her skirts in her hands, and hurried toward the house. Once inside, they all hastened toward the kitchen where the coachman and a gardener—who looked strikingly like Mrs. Audeley's butler in town—were enjoying a plate of oatcakes and parkins.

"What's this I hear, John?"

The retainers jumped to their feet in surprise. Apparently, the duke had not bothered to inform them that their mistress was on site.

"Gyles is not here?"

"No, Mrs. Audeley," said the coachman, tugging his forelock. "I was waiting in the box, ready to take him home the night of the ball at Lord Kendall's. But when he came out at last, he never climbed in and tells me instead to take the carriage back to Derbyshire as fast as possible without stopping at the townhouse."

"Was there a woman with him?"

"Aye," said John, looking down uncomfortably, "there was." It was not the sort of thing one liked to admit to a gentleman's mother.

Mrs. Audeley sighed and Lord Kendall guided her to a chair. "Now then, my good man," said the earl, "did you notice where Mr. Audeley and the young lady went?"

"Well, I thought it parlous strange, but as I was pulling away, they went and called for a hack. Mr. Gyles had a bag or bundle of some sort that he was carrying over his arm, and a small trunk, although I knows as it didn't belong to him, as I've never seen it in our carriage before."

"So, we've been following the wrong carriage all this time," said Mrs. Audeley.

"Confound it, yes!" said the duke. "But it's not as if they could have taken a hack all the way up to Scotland. They must have been headed somewhere nearby."

Lord Kendall cleared his throat, reminding them that there was no need to discuss all this in front of the servants. At his prompting, Mrs. Audeley led the way from the kitchen to the drawing room. "If I might be so bold," said Lord Kendall, "that note from Gyles might have clues."

"Oh," said Mrs. Audeley with a blush. "I think I left it in my reticule."

The lady did not have her reticule with her, but the Duke of Warrenton obliged by returning to the stables to retrieve the handbag from the carriage and bring the abandoned lady's maid into the house. Lord Kendall and Mrs. Audeley waited in awkward silence for him to return.

Mrs. Audeley wandered around the drawing room, putting cushions to rights and checking the dust on the mantelpiece that had accumulated in her absence. At last, she broke the silence. "It seems that you've been saved from offering for Lady Louisa."

"Indeed." Lord Kendall stood stiffly by the drawing room window, unable to sit until Mrs. Audeley did so.

After a few moments elapsed, Warrenton re-entered the room with the maid on his arm.

"Your reticule, ma'am." He deposited the bag in Mrs. Audeley's outstretched fingers. She fumbled with the strings and eventually extracted a letter.

Lord Kendall held out his right hand.

"It's really not very detailed—" began Mrs. Audeley, edging away from him.

But Lord Kendall was not to be denied. "I'm quite good at deciphering hidden meanings."

Inexorably, he drew the letter from Mrs. Audeley's fingers.

CHAPTER THIRTY-FOUR

The Return

Mother,

I have resolved to tender my services to Miss Lymington in her hour of need. It is impossible to think that I might be worthy of her, but if I can aid her in a permanent escape from her uncle, I shall be content.

It may be a long time till you see me again. I regret not being able to say good-bye or to give you my love. Ask Sir Abraham Hume to tend my Sweet-Scented China Rose. And should your own affairs reach a resolution in my absence, tell Lord Kendall he has my blessing.

Your Affectionate Son,

Gyles Audeley

Lord Kendall finished reading the letter and cast Mrs. Audeley a searching gaze. "An interesting conclusion."

"And wholly irrelevant to the matter at hand," retorted Mrs. Audeley. Clearly, Giles had been unaware of how presumptuous Lord Kendall had been when he penned that letter. She had had no time to explain to him the embarrassment of the earl's financial overreach.

"As fascinating as this conversation is," interrupted the Duke of Warrenton, "I think we must turn our attention to the fact that your son's hoodwinked us all by sending the carriage north. They could be holed up anywhere—London, Bath, Brighton. Louisa took enough jewels with her to pawn till doomsday, so she won't be hampered by lack of funds."

"Then you do not think they intend to marry?" asked Mrs. Audeley. "I thought Scotland was their only recourse with your niece being underage."

"So I thought when we were in London. I still have no doubt Louisa would marry if she felt she was out of options, but if she can find a way to wait out the next six months without leg-shackling herself to some nincompoop, perhaps that's the choice she'll take."

"I daresay that would be to Gyles' benefit," said Mrs. Audeley tartly, "as she is not at all the sort of girl who would make him a good wife."

Lord Kendall refolded the letter with decision and handed it back to Mrs. Audeley. "We must go back to London to retrace their steps. With your permission, that is."

Mrs. Audeley looked about in dismay. "I'm afraid you're right. But I must confess, I'm not looking forward to returning to town and facing Lady Comfort's rumours and insinuations. What a ramshackle woman everyone must think I am."

The duke took her hand and raised it to his lips. "If it would help, I could drop a word or two that you have behaved in an exceedingly virtuous manner all throughout our little visit to Derbyshire."

Lord Kendall glared at him.

Mrs. Audeley realised that the duke's comment, like so many of the more outrageous things he said, had been made solely to provoke a reaction from the stiffer members of society. "No, thank you, your grace," she said, pulling her hand away. "That would *not* help in the least."

Lord Kendall advanced toward Warrenton and spoke in a voice as chilly as a wine cellar. "I hope you will keep the existence of this excursion between ourselves, Warrenton, or I shall be very displeased."

"I'm sure I'll try," said the duke cheekily, "but Solomon Digby is going to be *very* curious. Where have I been, he'll ask, and who have I been consorting with? He's so in love with Louisa, you see, that he'll be insatiably insistent to know all the details of my search. Not to mention that he's already advanced me two thousand pounds in earnest money."

Lord Kendall snorted. "Two thousand pounds which you've already spent?"

The duke shrugged pathetically, as if fate had forced his hand throughout this entire affair. "He will take it ill indeed if I return without her."

"How ill?"

"Let's just say he has a pair of meaty looking footmen who look like they came to him by way of Seven Dials. I wouldn't relish running into them in a dark alley."

"Then why not stay here?" Mrs. Audeley voiced suddenly.

Both gentlemen stared at her.

"It's the perfect solution," she explained. "You've made London too hot to hold you, but you've no money to go anywhere else. You may stay at my house in Derbyshire, and I shall inform the servants that you are leasing the place while I remain in London. Lord Kendall and I can continue the search for Louisa in your stead. I doubt she will be amenable to rescuing your fortunes, but at least the delay will keep you out of Mr. Digby's clutches until his ire abates."

The Duke of Warrenton stared at Mrs. Audeley as if he were truly seeing her as a person for the first time. He rubbed his jaw with a thoughtful hand.

"Think on it for the night," urged Mrs. Audeley.

At this mention of imminent nightfall, Lord Kendall raised a new topic for discussion: he and Warrenton would put up at a nearby inn for propriety's sake. The duke pooh-poohed the idea roundly, but the earl would not be gainsaid. After a scanty dinner provided by the skeleton staff of retainers at the house, they departed for the night. Alone except for her retainers, Mrs. Audeley wandered outside to examine the care of the garden and assure herself that all was well with Gyles' pride and joy.

"And when will Mr. Audeley be back to see his roses?" asked Garrick's nephew.

"I don't know," his mistress replied pensively. "It may be a long while before we see him again."

The following morning, Mrs. Audeley saw that Jeanette had taken time to refresh her travelling gown. It smelled of rose water and lavender. The maid pinned her hair up in a simple chignon with a few curls about her face. "The simpler styles," she told Mrs. Audeley, "they make a lady look younger."

"I have no wish to appear other than I am," said Mrs. Audeley.

"You say that now," said the maid saucily, "but you would wish it if that uppity governess were here to distract the gentlemen." Clearly, Jeanette had a full understanding of what had taken them to Derbyshire and little liking for Miss Lymington.

The air was crisp and cold, but there was no rain. Warrenton walked over from the inn before Lord Kendall arrived in the carriage and found Mrs. Audeley in the breakfast room. "I've decided to accept your offer," he said in bright tones.

"I was hoping you might."

He helped himself to a plate of toasted muffins and bacon from the sideboard. "I must admit, Mrs. Audeley, when we first met in London, I considered you a ripe pigeon and a prime article, and I enjoyed the idea of putting Kendall's nose out of joint." He sat at the table, fork and knife in hand, and took a bite of the bacon. "But if you would permit it, I'd rather consider you a friend."

Mrs. Audeley's lips parted in surprise. "I would like that very much."

Warrenton smiled at her sheepishly, and she beamed her goodwill at him in return.

At that instant, Lord Kendall entered the breakfast room. His bright blue eyes darted from one face to the other. "Good morning," he said briskly.

"Are you hungry?" asked Mrs. Audeley, gesturing to the sideboard. She certainly did not want Lord Kendall to feel as if he had interrupted a private moment.

"No. I think we ought to get on the road as soon as possible."

"I won't be coming, Kendall," said Warrenton, continuing to tuck into his breakfast, "so you'll have Mrs. Audeley all to yourself in the carriage." He winked at the lady in question. She shook her head in exasperation.

"Fortunately, we still have Penelope's maid as a chaperone," said Lord Kendall dryly, "so we aren't forced to rely on your services."

"Oh, the French maid? I was hoping you could leave her here as company for me."

"Certainly not," said Mrs. Audeley. "You need to stop seeking out so much...company. Although I suspect that your character is far blacker in reputation than it is in fact."

"All smoke and no fire? Come now! I resent that," said the duke. "The next thing you'll be saying is that I'm as sterling a gentleman as Kendall."

Mrs. Audeley looked between the two of them, and though she was still piqued by Lord Kendall's effrontery, she could not lie. "I very much doubt that."

The earl might have his flaws, but his continued care for her wellbeing indicated that he was no Duke of Warrenton, just as his ability to admit himself in the wrong proved that he was no Mr. Audeley. If only he would reopen the conversation that had gone so poorly in his study four days ago—perhaps it was still the lingering memory of that kiss, but if the earl was able to offer some fuller sentiment than "I mean to marry you," she was quite willing to listen.

CHAPTER THIRTY-FIVE

Sentiments

THE RETURN TRIP TO London was even more fraught with tension than the trip to Derbyshire had been. The cloud of Gyles' disappearance still hung over them, and without Warrenton there to alternately needle and amuse the other travellers, an awkwardness hung over the carriage like a low fog.

Lord Kendall handled the horse changes and inn stops with competence and efficiency, maintaining a distant courtesy at all times. Often, Mrs. Audeley found herself wishing for a little more warmth in his manner, but she kept that private musing to herself. The rebuff she had given him at Kendall House had likely put all ideas of a romantic nature out of his head. She reminded herself that the cordiality of friendship was a far more level ground than the unequal arena of matrimony—although, at the moment, this ticklish truce they were both tiptoeing around could hardly be called cordial.

On the second evening of the return trip, in Alconbury, Lord Kendall bespoke a private parlour for their supper. "Would you like your maid to dine with us?"

"Jeanette went for a walk into the village—she said she needed air after so many days in the carriage. I daresay it would not be improper to dine alone."

Lord Kendall opened the door to the parlour and gestured for her to enter. "Certainly not. Especially since I told the innkeeper that you are my sister."

"Whatever for?"

"I had to have some excuse to pay for your lodging."

"Oh, goodness!" Mrs. Audeley clapped her hands to her cheeks which were turning as warm as the parlour fire. In the haste and worry of their journey, she had never thought about who was footing the bill for it. "I daresay you've paid for all the horses and the food and the inns for the whole of this trip." She folded her hands at her waist and lifted her chin determinedly. "I shall have my man of business come settle accounts with you when we return to London."

"That is quite unnecessary." Lord Kendall's chiselled jaw set into firm lines.

"Please, my lord. I insist."

"Mrs. Audeley," said Lord Kendall, pulling out the chair from the table to seat her, "you are an infuriatingly stubborn woman."

"And you, sirrah, are an infuriatingly dictatorial man." Mrs. Audeley took a seat in the chair.

"So, you've come round to Penny's way of thinking." Lord Kendall walked around to his own chair and began to decant the bottle of claret.

"It's true." Mrs. Audeley was tired of bandaging up her thoughts like a secret injury, and her words ran out with raw emotion. "You think you know what is best for everyone else, and then you manage, manage, manage everything without consideration for what others might want or how it might affect them."

"That is unfair. A gentleman can ease the way of those around him without being a selfish prig." As he spoke, he served her a helping of fillet of roasted pork.

Mrs. Audeley nodded her thanks for the food. "Is that what you've done? Eased the way for me?"

"That has been my intention."

"And yet, each of your actions has left me trammelled by rumours and trapped by assumptions."

Lord Kendall took a drink of the claret without taking his eyes off her face. Mrs. Audeley was struck by how brightly the colour blue could burn.

"Can't a man give a woman a gift simply because he admires her?"

"Only if a woman can receive a gift without insinuations being made and expectations being formed."

"No expectations. Only hopes. And whatever hopes I might have had were soundly dashed the night of Penelope's ball."

She looked askance at him.

"Have no fear, Mrs. Audeley. I shall not renew the sentiments that were so repugnant to you."

"What sentiments?" she demanded. "There were no sentiments—simply a declaration that you meant to marry me in order to salvage my reputation."

Lord Kendall looked taken aback. "Then I can only assume it was the kiss you disliked."

Mrs. Audeley stared at him, knife and fork in hand. "Again, Lord Kendall, the folly of making assumptions becomes apparent."

He fell silent at that, and they both fell to eating their dinner. The only sound was the crackling of the fire in the hearth. It was not until they had both finished eating and the innkeeper had cleared the dishes and gone away again that Lord Kendall again took the opportunity to speak.

"I have something to say to you, Mrs. Audeley, and it would oblige me greatly if you would listen to it all the way through before you respond."

CHAPTER THIRTY-SIX

Understanding

SINCE A PROTRACTED CONVERSATION was inevitable, Mrs. Audeley suggested that they remove from the table to the chairs beside the fire. Lord Kendall agreed, hoping that this was a sign his audience would be receptive.

"Now then," said Mrs. Audeley, once she was situated in an armchair with a warm quilt on her lap. "What was it you wanted to say, my lord?"

"You are prepared now to hear me pontificate?"

"One does like to be comfortable before enduring a pontification."

Lord Kendall cleared his throat. "Then I shall commence. I would have you know, Mrs. Audeley, that up until three months ago, I was fully convinced that I should live and die a bachelor. It was not because, as Penny says, no one would have me. Rather, I had spent my youth looking about myself, but no young lady had caught my interest.

"There was one season when I was almost caught—Lady Comfort's sister Miss Featherstone trapped me in a library and insisted I had compromised her. But my sister Caroline stood by me and claimed to have been present the whole time as our chaperone. Miss Featherstone's word could not hold up to Caroline's, and I was vindicated in the court of public opinion."

"I suppose that was the incident it took Lady Comfort so long to forgive."

"Indeed. She forbade Sir Oliver to associate with me for five years or more, and he—poor fool—obeyed her. I spent most of my twenties travelling between London, Bath, Brighton, Edinburgh, and then to the continent to visit Paris, Rome, Geneva, even Saint Petersburg. And in all those places there was no one that captured my imagination as the future Lady Kendall. Whenever I came to town, my mother and sister tried to match me with suitable young ladies. But every year the debutantes grew younger, and I grew inexorably older and wearier of the games the ton plays.

"Last year, when my sister Caroline died, my whole existence changed. I could no longer flit about like a gadfly. I had three young women depending upon me. I gave up town, the season, the hunting bungalows, and the house parties, and sequestered myself in Yorkshire. With Milly and Ginny, I found that I could win their trust easily enough, but Penelope was a different creature by far. She contradicted every statement I made and always assumed I had her worst interests at heart. When I resolved to bring her out for the season, she took umbrage and tried to run away. The rest you know.

"When we came to your house in Upper Cross, you gentled her with a word. It was like a skilled horse trainer with a skittish filly. You captured her affection that very afternoon, and I suppose it was then that you captured mine as well."

"I hardly think—"

"No, no!" Lord Kendall held up a hand to halt her. "I am a despot, you must remember, and I will not be interrupted."

Mrs. Audeley pressed her lips together firmly, but her eyes were twinkling as she made a sign for him to carry on.

"It was the way you took pity on Penelope's plight but saw reason at the same time. You have the rare gift, Mrs. Audeley, of sympathy mingled with good sense. Over the next couple months, I came to admire you more and more. I had never met a woman so eager to put others at their ease, so generous with her time and talent, and so capable with both the downstairs servants and society at large.

"As the days ran by till Penelope's ball, I found ways to spend more and more time in your company. The realisation that these halcyon days must, of necessity, soon come to an end added purpose and poignancy to each visit. I came to realise that my happiness depended entirely on hearing your laugh in the drawing room each day and seeing your charming face across the tea table.

"By the night of the ball, I had made up my mind that I would put a certain question to you. Imagine my surprise when you pre-empted me in the study with news that you were to leave on the morrow. I panicked and tried to salvage the situation with the only way I knew how, by offering a clear solution to the predicament that Lady Comfort's gossip had created. To my bafflement, you took offence at the solution. I feared that the sympathy and affection between us had been no more than the creation of my own lovesick mind."

Mrs. Audeley emitted a small cry of objection, but Lord Kendall raised a hand to indicate that he was not finished.

"Clearly, I failed to establish my reasons for wanting to marry you, so I will take a moment to do so now. You are kind. You are clever. And you are as pretty as a picture whether your gowns are new or old. Even if I had not thoughtlessly ruined your reputation through my careless behaviour, I would have still asked to marry you because I love you to distraction."

Lord Kendall had made the mistake of a precipitate kiss before. Three days ago in his study, to be exact. But he was a man who learned from his mistakes, and so he kept his distance from Mrs. Audeley and allowed her to make the next move.

"You...love me," she repeated cautiously.

"Yes, you are glorious."

Mrs. Audeley looked away at that tribute, and a soft flush of pink came over her cheeks. "Glorious for a woman of my age—"

"—for a woman of any age."

"But we must acknowledge the facts, Lord Kendall. I am advanced in years, and I would not be able to give you children."

"I don't care a jot about that. If I had wanted children, I should have married twenty years ago."

"But the earldom—"

"—will go to a distant cousin. And at that point I shall be dead and shan't have anything to complain about."

He looked at her pleadingly, but she stayed silent. He could sense that her defences had come down but that her will was still wavering. At that moment, Lord Kendall resolved to employ every ounce of stratagem he'd ever possessed.

"Perhaps I've bungled things too badly, though—"

"—not *too* badly."

"And I daresay you would hate having to care for Penny, Ginny, and Milly—"

"What fustian! I love your nieces."

"And I shouldn't wonder if you think me a brute like the late Mr. Audeley—"

"—Oh, I've reconsidered that notion."

"So, it's no surprise that you would reject my proposal again after I—"

"You foolish man! I'm not rejecting you."

"You're not?" Lord Kendall lifted his eyebrows.

"No," said Mrs. Audeley, flinging the quilt from her lap as if she had become overheated by the fire in the hearth.

"Well, in that case," said Lord Kendall, rising from his chair and moving closer. "If I may?"

"You may," she replied with a blush.

He extended a hand and raised her to her feet. One arm went around her waist, and with the other, he brushed the back of his knuckles against her cheek. "I have learned a great many things in life, Mrs. Audeley, but it pains me to say that I am still wholly ignorant of your Christian name."

"You are such a managing gentleman I would have thought you'd have managed to find it out by now." She peeped up at him beneath her eyelashes with a grin of good humour on her pink lips. "It's Rose."

"Well then, Rose Audeley, will you end my misery and do me the kindness of marrying me?"

"I will."

And this time their lips met with a tenderness and longing that was wholly unexpected to both of them, and they forgot both time and place as they melted into each other's arms in the inn parlour in Alconbury.

CHAPTER THIRTY-SEVEN

Uproar

THE FOLLOWING DAY WAS the last stage of the return journey to London. Lord Kendall, who had been such an advocate for propriety earlier, found himself wishing the French maid to Jericho more than once. As it was, he claimed the seat beside Mrs. Audeley, and they passed the hours with interlaced fingers and murmured asides while Jeanette smirked knowingly from the opposite side of the carriage.

It was late afternoon, just before dark, when the carriage rolled to a stop in front of Kendall House, the faint drizzle of November gleaming on the cobblestones. "Do you mind stopping here first?" asked Lord Kendall.

"Not at all. I'm anxious to know how the girls have got on in our absence."

They ascended the steps and were admitted by the butler, only to discover that the chaos in the entrance hall was shockingly similar to the morning they had left. Mrs. Haverstall had lost her characteristically unflappable calm, Ginny and

Milly were clutching at each other in a fountain of tears, and broad-chested Ned Haverstall was pacing back and forth in confusion.

"Kendall!" he cried. "Just the man we need."

Lord Kendall removed his gloves and hat and handed them to the butler while Mrs. Audeley gathered up the sobbing sisters into her arms. "What's amiss, Haverstall?"

"It's Miss Penelope," said the stocky gentleman. "The clouds cleared up a bit ago. Clarissa and the girls went out for a promenade in Hyde Park, and Miss Penny disappeared around the bend. Milly insists she was pulled into a curtained carriage and made off with."

"She *was*, Uncle Bertie!" said Milly. "She was abducted right in front of my eyes."

"Thunder and turf!" Lord Kendall reached for Milly and lifted her up into his arms. "Describe the carriage, Milly. What did it look like?"

"There was nothing special about it. It was painted black, and it had black horses."

"No symbols or coat-of-arms."

"No," wailed Milly.

"Who would have done such a thing?" asked Mrs. Haverstall to the room at large.

"I wonder," said Mrs. Audeley slowly, "if it could have anything to do with Solomon Digby."

"By Jove," said Lord Kendall, setting Milly down on the marble floor, "you might be right."

"He was furious at his reception here," continued Mrs. Audeley, "and he might have taken Penelope for revenge."

"Or if he thinks we're hiding Lady Louisa, perhaps he'll try to trade Penny for her," said Ginny, her eyes large with fright.

"Haverstall," said Lord Kendall with decision, "will you accompany me?"

"Of course," said Ned Haverstall grimly.

Lord Kendall took back the gloves and hat that he had just given the butler and put them on while Ned sent a footman for his own hat, gloves, and cane.

"What do you mean to do?" asked Mrs. Audeley quietly.

"Visit Digby's lodgings and tear the place apart," said Lord Kendall, his voice hoarse with emotion. He took her hand and squeezed it. "Reassure the girls that it will be all right."

Mrs. Audeley nodded and lifted her chin courageously.

"Pleased to see you again," said a loud, quavery voice from the hallway. Mrs. Gale had awoken from her nap in the library and was coming out into the entrance hall to see what all the commotion was. Trailing behind her was Mr. Richards who, in Lord Kendall's absence, had undertaken the organisation of Mrs. Gale as well as the organisation of the earl's daily correspondence.

"You as well," said Mrs. Audeley, doing her best to be loudly polite despite the inconvenience of the interruption.

"I see you've met my nephew. He's quite rich. Handsome too."

"Oh, indeed." Mrs. Audeley attempted a faint smile.

"I beg your pardon, Mrs. Gale," said Lord Kendall, "but I must be off to find Penelope. We shall talk later."

"But is not Miss Trafford here?" asked Mr. Richards. He took Mrs. Gale's elbow and guided her around the console table that her old eyes did not quite seem to see.

"No, unfortunately not."

Richards pointed past the place where the butler was standing and out the window towards the square. "Are you certain, my lord? There is a vehicle outside that appears to contain Miss Trafford."

Ginny and Milly rushed to press their noses against the narrow windows beside the front door. Lord Kendall's long legs were not far behind them. "Thunder and turf! It *is* Penny."

"Is that a phaeton?" asked Milly, staring open-mouthed at the high-perched contraption that swayed precariously to a halt in front of the door of Kendall House.

"Who is that gentleman beside Penny?" asked Ginny.

"That is what I mean to find out," said the earl sternly. "Stay here, girls."

Lord Kendall opened the front door and stepped out into the misty afternoon air. But before the door could shut again, Ginny, Milly, Mrs. Audeley, and the Haverstalls spilled out onto the steps behind him, too worried to keep themselves inside the doors of the respectable townhouse.

"Oh, Uncle Bertie, you're home!" cried Penny, standing up in the seat of the high-perch phaeton. She turned to the fair-haired, square-jawed gentleman holding the reins. "Hand me down from this contraption this instant."

CHAPTER THIRTY-EIGHT

Abduction

THE LIVERIED TIGER IN the back of the phaeton jumped down and ran forward to take the horses' heads. The driver leapt gracefully over the side and, seizing the impatient Penny about the waist, lifted her down onto the cobblestones.

"Landsdowne," Lord Kendall uttered sharply. "What is the meaning of this?"

The fair-haired viscount jutted out his square chin with annoyance. "I set out to do you a favour, Kendall, but I must say, it's been almost more trouble than it's worth."

"Penny!" shrieked the girls, clutching at their returned sister. "Where have you been?"

"Oh, you will never guess the perils I have encountered this afternoon!"

Penelope put a hand to her forehead in a dramatic gesture, and Mrs. Audeley reached for her to fold her into a quick embrace.

"What happened?" demanded Lord Kendall, too tense with emotion to speak gently.

"We were out for a promenade in Hyde Park, and I went ahead of Mrs. Haverstall and the girls since they were walking unpardonably slowly. When I came around some shrubbery, there was a black carriage standing by, and a rough fellow—I think he was the coachman—grabbed me by the arms and shoved me inside like I was a bag of flour or a bundle of carpet.

"The curtains were drawn inside, but I could make out the voice of that loathsome Mr. Digby. He grabbed me and pinioned my arms so that I was forced to sit right up against him, and then he started to spout all sorts of nonsense about how he was going to enjoy tying *me* up."

"Oh, Penny!" gasped Ginny. "How perfectly awful."

"Yes, well, he seemed particularly sore about Lady Louisa having escaped his clutches and said that if he couldn't find her, he was going to make do with me as I was *almost* as pretty as she is."

Here, Penelope's lip began to quiver. Lord Kendall's eyebrows lifted, and he caught Mrs. Audeley's eye. They could only pray that it was Penny's vanity that had suffered the most during this adventure.

"I tried to elbow his fat stomach, but he would not let go of me with his meaty hands, and after ten or fifteen minutes, we arrived at a den of iniquity."

Lord Kendall looked at the viscount for clarification. "Janson's," said the gentleman in low tones, by which he meant a lower-order gaming house in Piccadilly.

"Surely, the place was empty at this time of day?" asked Lord Kendall.

"Yes," said Penny, "but Mr. Digby seemed to have some sort of arrangement with the proprietor, and he had his despicable coachman haul me out of the carriage and into one of the rooms in the back."

Mrs. Haverstall gasped, and Mrs. Audeley sent up a silent prayer that this tale would turn in a better direction than it was tending. Lord Kendall interrupted the story. "Penny, I think you may finish this tale later, in the house, in private—no need to stand out on the street discussing it."

"Oh, but I'm almost finished," said Penelope, waving off his concern. "Mr. Digby tied me to a chair, and he was just about to gag me with a curtain tie—he thought that very amusing as the same had been done to him—when I told him that there was a pebble in my half-boot and would he please unlace it as it was hurting my foot horribly."

"Penelope!" gasped Mrs. Audeley.

Lord Kendall's chiselled jaw began to twitch uncontrollably.

"He seemed to find that incredibly amusing too, and he knelt down to unlace my boot, and while he was distracted with locating my ankle under my petticoats, I kicked him as hard as I could with my other boot."

"In the head?" asked Milly breathlessly.

"In the head," confirmed Penelope, her black curls bouncing with vigour. "And he gave a little groan and passed out unconscious right in front of me."

Mrs. Audeley heard Viscount Landsdowne muttering and thought she could make out something about a very wicked pair of trim ankles.

"But what did you do next?" asked Ginny. "How did you escape?"

"I was still tied to the chair, and I was a little afraid that the odious coachman would come back, but I took a chance and began to call for help—"

"At which point I overheard Miss Trafford's cries, located her, and removed her from the premises," said the viscount.

"That's casting yourself in a very favourable light," said Penelope with a sniff. She looked at her uncle appealingly. "He untied me and told me to be quiet—quite rudely, too. And then made me follow him back through a maze of rooms in this den of iniquity. And whenever we passed a waiter or a servant, he called me Miss Molly and said he was going to take me home to my house in Cheapside. Even though he knew very well exactly who I was!"

Viscount Landsdowne shook his head. "The idiot girl would not stop announcing to the whole world that she was Miss Trafford."

"And then he threw me up into the seat of this harum-scarum contraption"—Penelope gestured contemptuously to the high-perch phaeton standing behind them—"and hurtled down the streets at an alarming pace. I thought we should careen into a carriage or a wagon more than once."

The viscount gritted his teeth. "I was trying to restore you to the bosom of your family as swiftly as possible, Miss Trafford. Before you could do more damage to your reputation by being seen about London without a suitable chaperone."

"Yes, well, perhaps it might have been more discreet to call a hack," said Mrs. Audeley.

"And leave my greys tied up at Janson's? I think not."

"Whatever the case," said Lord Kendall, "this conversation must come off the street immediately. Landsdowne, might I have a word with you in my study?"

The young viscount nodded, likely having been aware that such an interview would be forthcoming. He gave orders to his tiger to walk the horses while they were waiting. Mr. and Mrs. Haverstall began shepherding the younger two girls back up the steps while Mrs. Audeley took Penny's arm affectionately.

Lord Kendall's butler held the front door open, but before the family and visitors could troop inside, a closed carriage, travelling swiftly into the square came to a halt not ten feet from the waiting phaeton. The carriage door opened and out stepped Sir Oliver and Lady Comfort, the latter of whom was clearly brimming with outrage that was soon to be spilled.

CHAPTER THIRTY-NINE

Ultimatum

"Hallo there, Kendall," said Sir Oliver, fingering his watch fob nervously.

"Lord Kendall," said Lady Comfort imperiously. "A word if you please."

"Very well," said Lord Kendall, his own glacial expression freezing some of her arrogance. "But I will not wrangle with you in the street for all of Grosvenor Square to hear. Come inside and make your complaint, for I assume that's what I have to look forward to."

The entire party made their way up the steps and into the house, entering the large drawing room where Mr. Richards had just manoeuvred Mrs. Gale into a seat by the window. Discreetly, the Haverstalls and the secretary tiptoed away into the corridor, leaving the family to sort out events without a larger audience.

"Sit down, please," said Lord Kendall, and within seconds the couches and armchairs were filled with Comforts and Traffords while the Viscount Landsdowne took up a stance by the hearth and Mrs. Audeley moved towards the door to murmur instructions to the butler.

"Now then, Lady Comfort," said Lord Kendall, seating himself in the brass-studded chair in the middle of the gathering. "What do you want to say?"

Lady Comfort sniffed. "As a friend, I have information helpful for an inexperienced guardian to young ladies. I came to inform you that Miss Trafford has been spotted driving down Piccadilly with Viscount Landsdowne in an open vehicle with her dress in disarray. But I see you already know all about it." She turned meaningfully to the young lady in question and looked her up and down disdainfully. "No doubt your niece is modelling her hoydenish behaviour on the...*ladies* with whom she has been thrown into company since her arrival in London." She fixed her eye on Mrs. Audeley.

"What Arabella means to say, Kendall," added Sir Oliver, looking at the tops of his boots. "is that certain worlds aren't meant to mix. You're certainly entitled to have your fun, but keep it confined to a snug little bungalow in Kent. When you let your affairs of the heart run rampant, it's confusing to young ladies what's what and who's what, if you know what I mean."

"I'm afraid that I don't," said Lord Kendall. "Could you be less obtuse?" He crossed one leg over the other and drummed his fingers against the leg of his buff-coloured pantaloons, prepared to wait until his friends elucidated their complaints.

"But surely, Kendall," hissed Lady Comfort, "we cannot speak freely in front of such delicate young flowers."

"Oh, don't mind us," said Ginny, squished into one armchair along with Milly.

"We're quite able to follow the conversation," offered the youngest Trafford.

"It appears you think that Penny is becoming a sad romp because of all the time she spends with Mrs. Audeley," continued Ginny, "although why you should think that is beyond me."

"Indeed," said Milly. "Mrs. Audeley has *never* let herself get abducted or thrown harum-scarum into a high perch phaeton."

"Abducted!" echoed Lady Comfort.

"'Pon my word, Kendall," said Sir Oliver. "What's the girl going on about? Why would Landsdowne abduct someone?"

"If I may," interjected Viscount Landsdowne. "The facts of the matter are that Miss Trafford and her sisters were taking a promenade, properly chaperoned as you would expect of meek and gently bred young ladies." His nostrils flared as he stated those descriptors. "They were set upon by cutpurses, and I was able to offer my services in driving off the malefactors. In the uproar, Miss Trafford turned her ankle, and so it seemed prudent to bring her home in the phaeton rather than making her walk."

Sir Oliver blinked. "Egad!"

Penny, bewildered by such a garbled rendition of her adventure, opened her mouth to correct the mendacious story, but Mrs. Audeley had anticipated such a circumstance. Before Penny could recite a fuller version of events and give Lady Comfort even more fodder for gossip, Mrs. Audeley interrupted. "Goodness, here is the tea tray. I daresay everyone could use a cup of warm tea and a slice of cake." She gestured for the butler to place the tea tray on the low table in front of the settee.

Lady Comfort rose to her feet, reaching for her husband's hand and drawing him up to a standing position as well. "Absolutely not. I will not be served tea at Kendall House by a common stale."

"Eh? What's that?" asked Mrs. Gale from her seat at the window. "The tea cake is stale?"

Lord Kendall rose from his chair. "Arabella, you have known me for a long time, and there is a certain freedom of manner that is permitted to friends. But this—this is beyond the pale. If you wish me to acknowledge you in society, you will apologise to the future Lady Kendall immediately."

Lady Comfort gasped and pressed her hands to her heart as if overcome by palpitations.

"Future Lady Kendall," blustered Sir Oliver. "Come now, Bertie, this won't fadge."

"Oh!" cried the Trafford girls in chorus.

"Mrs. Audeley is to be our aunt?" said Milly.

"How divine!" cooed Ginny.

"What a good thing that Uncle Bertie didn't marry that horrid Lady Louisa," said Penelope, "as some were suggesting he ought."

All three girls crowded around Mrs. Audeley, begging to be told the details of the betrothal.

Meanwhile, Lord Kendall drew his censorious friends over to the door of the drawing room and fixed a stern eye on both of them. "Well, what's it to be? Shall I cut you dead at the next assembly, or will you make your apologies to my bride?"

Sir Oliver cleared his throat. "'Pon rep, you've simply caught us off our guard you have. Who would have thought—"

"It will be the scandal of the year," declared Lady Comfort, unwilling to budge an inch, "to flaunt your mistress in front of the ton and then marry her. Your nieces' reputations will all be tainted by it."

Lord Kendall leaned in closer, and his voice grew dark with warning. "The only reason anyone thinks she *is* my mistress is because of your poisonous tongue."

Lady Comfort hissed at him like a feral cat, and had she been possessed of a tail, the hair on it would have bristled all over. Trying to maintain as much dignity as she could muster, she arched her back and exited the drawing room, leaving her husband behind.

Sir Oliver's eyes grew large. "I say, so she's not...? You're not...?"

"No."

"Can't say as I would have blamed you," said Sir Oliver lamely. "She's a tempting armful, and too pleasant to curdle the milk at the breakfast table."

Lord Kendall looked at him disdainfully. "That's hardly an apology, Oliver."

"Yes, well, I'm sorry, but you know how it is...." He looked over to the empty place where Lady Comfort had been standing. "I have to toe the line and do as I'm told or there'll be the devil to pay."

"Very well then," said Lord Kendall. "Then consider our connection severed. I won't endeavour to repair it this time. Good day to you." Without another word, he turned his back on Sir Oliver and refused to look his direction as the henpecked husband shuffled his way to the door.

Chapter Forty

Romance

AFTER THE UNGENEROUS DEPARTURE of Sir Oliver and Lady Comfort, Lord Kendall disappeared to the study with the viscount while Mrs. Audeley gathered the girls around her in the drawing room. Milly climbed onto her lap and the other two girls took up positions on either side of her on the settee.

"How soon are you to be married?" asked Ginny.

"I don't know," said Mrs. Audeley. "We haven't had the chance to discuss it, but I imagine it shall be as soon as possible."

"Good," said Penny, "then you can put that horrid Lady Comfort in her place. The only thing I'm sad about is that if Uncle Bertie cuts them in society, shall I be obliged to cut Cassie too?"

"I don't know—I'm sure your uncle can explain it to us later and tell us how we ought to behave."

"Will we stay in London?" asked Milly.

"Yes, for a while at least." Mrs. Audeley felt tears begin to well up in her eyes, but she contained them and smiled bravely. "We did not find Gyles, and so we must search for him some more. He may still be in town. And besides," she said, trying to brighten the mood, "there is your season to think about, Penny."

"Oh, yes," said Penny, looking at the floor as a shadow came over her face.

"What is it, my dear?" said Mrs. Audeley, taking her hands in hers.

Penny wrinkled her nose. "It's just that Gyles is gone because he prefers Lady Louisa to me. And Viscount Landsdowne told me that...that he only opened the ball with me as a favour to Uncle Bertie." Her lip began to quiver. "D-do you think I might be an...antidote!"

"Certainly not," said Mrs. Audeley loyally. "You are a trifle melodramatic at times, but you are a lovely girl and someday soon you will attract just the right gentleman to make your heart sing."

"Is that what Uncle Bertie does?" asked Ginny. "Make your heart sing?"

Mrs. Audeley opened her mouth to answer, but Penny interrupted. "Oh, we shouldn't expect that, Ginny. Feelings are different when you are old. And besides, Uncle Bertie is wholly incapable of romance."

Mrs. Audeley shut her mouth. Some things were not worth explaining.

"Was the cake stale?" asked a loud voice from the window. During the uproar at Lady Comfort's comments and the aftermath of her departure, the earl's cousin had been left to her own devices.

"Mrs. Gale," said Mrs. Audeley, gently lifting Milly off her lap. "How could we have forgotten about you? I will serve you your tea right away." She made a plate for the earl's cousin's wife and plates for the girls too. By this time, the news of the engagement had spread from the butler through the downstairs to the whole of the house. Mrs. Haverstall returned to the drawing room to offer her friend sincere congratulations.

"Are you happy?" she asked searchingly.

"Very much so," said Mrs. Audeley. "You must forget everything I said in the carriage the other night. Lord Kendall is a gentleman of the highest calibre and quite able to express all the right sentiments when the occasion presents itself."

"I'm glad," said Clarissa Haverstall, pressing her friend's hand.

"Thank you for keeping the girls safe while we were in Derbyshire."

"If only I had truly done so, but thank God for Viscount Landsdowne and his protection of Miss Trafford. If you should need more help searching for Gyles, Ned would be happy to oblige. It would give him something to do, and I think you'll find that gentlemen are the happiest when they have a project to occupy themselves."

"What's this?" asked Lord Kendall, who had just re-entered the drawing room. "I'll have you know that I'm in no need of projects, Mrs. Haverstall. I intend to occupy myself with my new bride for the foreseeable future."

Mrs. Audeley blushed at that and gave him a private look.

Mrs. Haverstall, perceptive as always, gathered up the girls and led them out of the drawing room to help her pack her things so she could return home that evening. In the corner,

Mrs. Gale had fallen asleep again, her saucer and cup balanced precariously on the stomacher of her old-fashioned dress.

"How was your interview with Viscount Landsdowne?" asked Mrs. Audeley as they sat down together upon the settee.

"Excellent. I never hear better sense from anyone than Andrew Wilmot. He offered to handle Digby's punishment himself so that I can be removed from the situation. Hopefully, it will keep Penelope's name from being mentioned in the affair."

"What was the viscount doing at Janson's in the first place?"

"He didn't say, but surely a gentleman's secrets are his own." He reached for her hand.

"Except from his future wife, you mean." She looked at him archly as his fingers travelled lightly up her forearm.

"I have no secrets from you. Now I shall tell you quite openly each time I spend money on your wardrobe or give you my mother's jewellery. Not," he said carefully, "because I wish to control you, but because I adore you."

"How very romantic, Lord Kendall." She tilted her head sideways as she looked at him, and a sparkle came into her eye. "And yet Penelope assures me that her uncle is wholly incapable of romance."

"Penny is a Very. Silly. Girl," he said, pulling her closer and punctuating each word with a kiss on her eyebrows and forehead. His lips lowered to her mouth, and they spent the next several moments taking full advantage of Mrs. Gale's snores from the other side of the drawing room.

Finally, as the clock struck seven, they reluctantly pulled apart, knowing that dinner was soon to be served and the rest of the family would be returning. "How long till we can marry?" asked Lord Kendall, breathing heavily. "Must we wait till Gyles is found?"

"N-no," said Mrs. Audeley slowly, "since I know that we have his blessing. He is of age. Perhaps I must be content to let him sort out matters with Lady Louisa on his own. But it will be at least three weeks till we can marry since the banns must be said."

Lord Kendall rose to his feet and offered her his arm. "Hmm, I must tell you, my dear, that I believe that your choice to turn aside at Grantham and continue west to Derbyshire was a strategic error."

"Is that so?" asked Mrs. Audeley, raising her own eyebrows to match his. "Is that because you think we would have actually found Gyles at the Scottish border?"

"No, no," said Lord Kendall, giving her a cheeky smile as he led her through the doors and out into the corridor. "But we were so close to Scotland that we might have made use of an anvil parson ourselves. Then we could already be married tonight instead of waiting three weeks!" He looked at her ardently, his blue eyes sparking heat like a flintstone. "And even though I may be too old for romance, I can tell you truthfully that they will be the three longest weeks of my life."

Epilogue

IT WAS A NINE days' wonder in the metropolis when the story of Lord Kendall's betrothal to a nobody from Derbyshire made the rounds. Rumour reigned supreme. Lady Comfort's gossip about Mrs. Audeley's unsavoury past with *both* the Duke of Warrenton and the Earl of Kendall was repeated from house to house. More than a few declared that they would not admit such a fast and notorious creature into their social circle, regardless of whether Kendall tied the knot with her or not.

But soon, the lowly but well-liked Mrs. Haverstall paid a round of calls and let it be known that Lady Comfort was still smarting from Lord Kendall's snub of her family two decades earlier. As older and wiser heads recalled the past scandal, they concluded that just as Miss Featherstone's story had proven spurious back then, so Lady Comfort's claims were doubtless spurious now. It was a case of sour grapes as old as Aesop himself.

And when it was seen how pleasant and unassuming the Derbyshire widow was, the tide of public opinion changed altogether. By the time the wedding occurred during the first week of December, Mrs. Audeley was already on her way to being the darling of the ton while Lady Comfort had lost much of her cachet.

St. Paul's saw the solemnisation of the marriage vows, and Kendall House hosted the wedding breakfast immediately following. The house was filled with friends and well-wishers, and whenever someone complimented Lord Kendall on the delightful table of meat pies, fruit pastries, and plum cakes, he informed them that it had nothing to do with him as "his secretary had made all the arrangements."

The Haverstalls agreed, once again, to chaperone the girls while the newlyweds took a wedding trip to Cornwall. Mr. Digby was no longer in town—due to circumstances spoken of in hushed tones when only gentlemen were present—but Lady Kendall still made each of the girls promise not to leave Mrs. Haverstall's side for even a minute when venturing outside the walls of the house.

Three days after the wedding, Lord and Lady Kendall departed. Not five minutes after the carriage wheels rolled down the street, a knock came on the door. The Trafford girls gathered at the stair railing and watched curiously as the butler admitted a lean old fellow with a fringe of white hair along the sides of his balding head.

"Sir Abraham Hume, at your service," said the visitor, listening patiently as Mrs. Haverstall explained that the woman he had come to call on was not currently in residence. "Ah, well," he said, "if Lady Kendall is not here, at least the rosebush is, yes?"

Penelope hurried down the stairs to assist Mrs. Haverstall with the visitor. "You mean Gyles' rosebush?"

"Indeed. The Sweet-Scented China Rose that I gave clippings of to Mr. Audeley two summers ago."

"It's in the central courtyard by the stables," said Mrs. Haverstall.

"I'm not sure that Gyles would care for it to be shown," objected Penelope.

"You are quite right to be protective of such a rare species," said Sir Abraham. "But I have here in my pocket a letter from Mr. Audeley instructing me to look in on the rosebush and take possession of it should I feel that it needs more expert tending."

"A letter? From Gyles?" Penelope's mouth fell open in shock. "Oh, please, good sir, may we read it."

"Of course, of course," replied Sir Abraham, and after a bit of searching through his pockets, he located the folded piece of paper and allowed Penelope to peruse it.

"See here, Mrs. Haverstall," said Penelope, "the postmark is less than a week ago. And you'll never guess where it was posted from."

"Where?"

"France! Gyles has gone to France."

From the top of the staircase, Ginny and Milly let out a squeal of surprise. Mrs. Haverstall gasped and put a hand to her heart.

"Yes, I did think that a bit odd," said Sir Abraham, "given the current state of relations with the Frenchies. But perhaps he's in search of a rare species of flower. One makes sacrifices for the sake of botanical knowledge."

"Romantical, not botanical," muttered Penelope, but Sir Abraham missed the import of that statement.

"Does Gyles say anything important in the letter?" asked Mrs. Haverstall. "You must understand, Sir Abraham, that it has been some time since we have heard from him, so every word is precious."

"No," said Penelope, her eyes flicking swiftly over the page. "It's all about grafting and pollinating and mulching and irrigating. What a lot of fusty terms and tedious questions. There's no word here of whether he's married or not, or even if he's still with *her*."

"Married?" asked Sir Abraham, bewildered but still trying to follow the conversation. "Am I to understand that there are felicitations in store for Mr. Audeley?"

"That," said Penelope, "remains to be seen." She folded the letter back up and returned it to Sir Abraham. "And even if he *is* married, I'm not sure that felicitations are the correct response on our part..."

FINIS

Books

by Rosanne E. Lortz

Pevensey Mysteries

To Wed an Heiress

The Duke's Last Hunt

A Duel for Christmas

Allen Abbey Romances

The Gentleman in the Ash Tree

The Lady in the Moneylender's Parlour

The Vicar and the Village Scandal

Kendall House Regency Romances

The London Rose

The Paris Footman

Comfort Quartet

A Brother's Wager

Sketches by the Serpentine

Made in United States
North Haven, CT
30 January 2025